Tahitian Sunset Rose

Other Books by Stacey Lynn Schlegl:
    Greener Pastures
    Wishing

Children's Book:
    Little Frog

Tahitian Sunset Rose

a novel by
Stacey Lynn Schlegl

RHP

This book is a work of fiction. Names, characters, places and incidents are either product of the author's imagination or are used fictitiously. Any resemblance to actual events, locales, persona, living or dead, is entirely coincidental.

TAHITIAN SUNSET ROSE

All Rights Reserved © 2008 by Stacey Lynn Schlegl

Cover Art and Design by CH Creations
Interior Design by CH Creations

No part of this book may be reproduced or transmitted in any form or by any means, electronic or mechanical, including photocopying, recording, or by information storage and retrieval system except by a reviewer who may quote brief passages in a review to be printed in a magazine or newspaper without written permission from the author.

Published June 2008
RoseHeart Publishing
www.roseheartbooks.com

ISBN 10: 0-9801504-3-4
ISBN 13: 978-0-9801504-3-8

Printed in the United States of America

For my Mom, my Dad, my two beautiful children and my sister, Lisa, who all have supported my writing...and especially my husband, Paul, who loves me in sickness and health until death do us part.

Also, for all those people our there thinking their marriage is over, to those that are battling illness and to everyone just looking for a happy ending. I wish you many beautiful sunsets and the happy ending you deserve.

One

Becky couldn't even clench her teeth against the clamor. It was like a woodpecker hitting a microphone and the receiving end was in her ear. Her head pounded with the annoyingly deafening beat. Her foot itched, but she wasn't allowed to scratch it. Her nose had a tickle, too but no scratching or moving. She could hear her own breath, amazing despite the noise. It was shallow, coming in quick hard puffs. If an observer said she was hyperventilating, she'd probably agree.

Her mind searched and found the only other time she was about to hyperventilate. It was like her brain was trying to grasp at something to focus on rather than the place she was currently at. Her mind found the old memory way in back in the filing cabinet as if on survival mode. The file it pulled was a time when she had just turned thirteen and was at the county fair back home. She and her girlfriends were waiting in line for the Ferris wheel. The attendant's snake tattoo on his arm danced as he motioned them to step forward. The bar of the Ferris wheel chair was caught like a fly in his spider web-decorated hand.

"Come on!" he grumbled with his beady eyes on her friends. He then spit a stream of tobacco juice onto the ground, almost hitting their shoes.

Andrea, Tammy Jane and Carmen jumped into one seat with grins on their faces. The bar closed on their laps and the tattoo-covered man pushed a button, sending the chair up into the air and another empty one down for Becky.

She was left standing all alone. She yelled up at Tammy Jane, "Why did you all leave me here?"

"There wasn't room for four!" Tammy Jane shouted back and waved from her perch. Why didn't they go two and two like they'd talked about? Why would her friends leave her at the last minute?

The carnival worker spewed another rivulet of brown liquid into the dirt and gave her a dirty leer. He reminded her of a spitting cobra but less friendly. She fidgeted and tried to stand as tall as her five-foot eight frame would allow.

"Come on, you pretty young thing, Big Bart don't bite … not unless you want me to."

Becky backed up a step. She could see his eyes staring at her small-developing breasts. She backed up another step and found herself tripping over someone's shoe.

She felt arms catch her with ease and after she managed to steady herself again, she turned around to apologize. "I'm so sorry. I…"

"That's all right. My big feet get stepped on all the time on the basketball court. Do you need someone to ride with?" he asked, nodding toward Tammy Jane, Carmen and Andrea dangling their feet in the air.

Becky could almost taste the oversized pickle that Andrea had dared her to eat before getting on the Scrambler. She'd made it through the spinning and churning Octopus ride keeping the pickle down, but all of a sudden, it threatened to come up.

"I…I…my friends…" Becky didn't know what to say so she pointed to the three soon to be ex-friends now leaning forward and waving happily at her from above, Carmen's braces reflecting the festival's lights.

"Well, I'd be happy to ride with you … if you want."

She didn't know what to do. The boy she had been staring at for the entire day, which she was dying to talk to but was too scared, was asking to go on a ride with her.

The tattoo man shouted, making the alligator inked on his jaw open and close its sharp teeth. "Get on or get out of line!" It was almost as if the tattoo man was jealous of his new competition.

Becky hesitated for a second more and then she found herself nodding in affirmation.

"Is that a yes?" the boy asked.

"Yes…" she managed to squeak out in a breathy voice. She felt like she was going to hyperventilate from being so close to the boy of her dreams. She could play basketball in front of an entire gymnasium full of chanting fans, ride any ride after eating jumbo dill pickles and hotdogs loaded with mustard, ketchup and pickles, but heaven forbid she had to sit next to someone so unbelievably cute.

Carmen called down, "Enjoy your ride."

All of her friends were grinning smugly. She could tell by their faces that leaving her behind had been obviously planned. They knew she liked this boy and they must've seen him step into line at the last minute. Why hadn't she noticed? She supposed she was too busy chatting with her friends and ironically, daydreaming about the very guy that was in line right behind her.

Becky strode forward and sat down in the seat. The boy she had ogled all day sat next to her. Their thighs touched and she jolted like she had been jabbed by someone who had rubbed their feet across a carpet and then shocked her. It felt like where they were touching was energized by electricity. She tried to scoot over, but the small metal bench didn't give her room. How in the heck did Carmen, Andrea and Tammy Jane all fit in one seat? She looked over at her Ferris wheel companion. She supposed he made up two of them in girth. He was wide in the shoulders and had long basketball-attractive legs.

Did he like her? Did he feel the heat in his leg like she felt in hers from the touch?

"Ready?" He smiled showing the most perfect teeth. It was the kind of teeth that took most people years of braces and dental work to attain. She'd just gotten her own braces off a month ago. She was silently thanking her mother for getting an early start on that process. What if she'd met her dream boy with braces? She heard horror stories from girls that got cut from boy's braces while kissing and vice versa.

"Um… sure… no problem," Becky managed to say, despite her nervousness from being this close to him. She usually liked boys that had dark hair, but for some reason, she found his red hair so unbelievably adorable.

Riding that Ferris wheel was like a dream. Everything seemed so surreal. She remembered answering his questions, but had no idea if her answers made sense or not. She also remembered his hand almost touching hers, but not quite.

After she got off the Ferris wheel, she mumbled a quick 'thank you', dragging her friends off to the opposite end of the park. Carmen was so mad that all their hard work and planning didn't pay off in a date with the red-haired boy or at least a few more rides, she let her feelings be known.

"He liked you!" Carmen yelled. "Why else would he just suddenly pop behind you in line? Are you that clueless to the ways of the opposite sex? You can get an 'A' in any science and math class, but be darned if you can't understand something so obvious and straightforward. He's been watching you the entire fair and just 'happened' to stand in the same line as you… gee… hmm… rocket science?" Carmen said sarcastically.

Becky shook her head. "I understand all right. What I understand is that it was nothing more than pure coincidence that he was behind me in line, and his saying 'yes' to riding with me was nothing more than him just feeling sorry for me because you all ditched me. He was taking pity on the pathetic damsel in distress. It was nothing more."

"He did not just take pity on you. He liked you! You should've seen how he looked at you the entire time. His eyes never left you," Carmen rebuked.

Carmen was one of her best friends, but they always seemed to clash on ideas and thoughts. Her friend was very strong in her opinions and very vocal about them. Becky was equally independent and didn't appreciate being talked to in this manner.

"You're imagining things," Becky denied, nearly losing her temper.

"I saw it, too," Andrea piped in.

"Me too," Tammy Jane echoed.

"All of you are seeing things," Becky remarked stubbornly, as they moved over to stand in line for the Octopus ride for the third time that day.

"Proof. We all saw the same thing. Now he probably thinks you hate him because you left him standing in the dirt staring at you running off!" Carmen exclaimed, a hand on her hips, green eyes flashing at her friend. Even her freckles seemed angry.

"Let's just enjoy the festival…" Becky murmured, trying to change the subject.

"For being so brave and confident all the time, you sure are chicken when it comes to following your heart and taking a risk with your feelings," Tammy Jane pointed out as only a best friend could.

"I'm not chicken, I'm cautious," Becky defended, still feeling her breath coming in shallow puffs when she thought of her close encounter on the Ferris wheel with a feeling she just didn't understand.

The noise stopped and a soothing voice spoke into her ear,

"You've just completed one set of pictures. You can move only your arms, and if you want, you can cough. No moving your head or any other part of your body."

Her itch on her foot didn't matter because she couldn't sit up to reach it. Becky did scratch her nose quickly and then said without moving her jaw or lips at all, "I'm ready for the next round." She felt like a ventriloquist.

"Okay, now relax. You're doing great. I'll put on some special music to help you with all the racket," the comforting voice told her.

"How much longer?" Becky asked. It felt like eternity inside of this medical cage.

"Thirty-five minutes more," the soft voice drawled, "and just for the record, for being claustrophobic, you're doing great."

"Thanks," Becky managed to get out.

The music started to play, the song very familiar. She smiled inside despite the fear coursing through her veins. Her thoughts went back to a time so long ago when that song played…

The soft ballad of REO Speedwagon's *'I Can't Fight This Feeling'* poured out of the radio. Becky sat on the carpet in her red boxers and flowered shirt holding the phone to the speakers with a determined set jaw. She hoped that Andrea didn't notice her basketball fuzzy slippers quaking. The song ended and her friend frantically motioned her to say something into the phone.

Becky could hear a boy's voice saying something, but she couldn't tell what it was because she was holding the phone still in midair. Andrea shook her arms again, looking quite silly. She hesitantly put the phone up to her lips ready to say something, but then suddenly didn't feel as brave as she did when she first took the dare. She panicked.

Andrea sprang to her feet as only a seasoned cheerleader could do and yanked the phone toward her and yelled for the caller to hear, "She'll meet you after school tomorrow in the gym on the basketball court!"

Becky gave her best friend an angry glare and jerked the phone back and slammed it on the hook. Anger allowed her to find her voice and she yelled, "I'm not meeting him! Then he'll know it was me that called him. I have biology with him, for goodness sake."

"Life is short. You need to take a chance and live a little." Andrea's voice was barely a whisper and her friend turned her head. All Becky saw was a blonde braid flipping in the air.

She walked over and put a hand on Andrea's shoulder. "I'm sorry for yelling."

"I'm sorry I upset you," Andrea said with tears in her big blue eyes.

"It's nothing that a container of cookie dough ice cream and two spoons can't solve." Becky gave her friend a reassuring grin.

Normally she would've put her friend on silence probation for an hour of the sleepover for such a stunt, but Becky could tell this wasn't the time for teenage antic punishments—it was the time to just be friends and eat ice cream. And to be completely honest, a secret part of her wanted to give Andrea a high five for pushing her to something she normally wouldn't have had the courage to do—meet her crush.

The next day, Becky almost didn't show up on the basketball court to give away her secret song-playing identity, however, Andrea forced her to go ... literally. She dragged Becky down the hallway of the high school until her feet were on the free-throw line. Before she had a chance to hightail it out of the sock-smelling arena, in walked a handsome red-haired boy with a smile. He was just as handsome as the first time she noticed him when she was thirteen at the fair. Becky swallowed hard and tried to act like she was cool, calm and adult-like as possible—since she was now much older at the ancient age of fifteen. She laughed inside at the thought of being old. Someone 'old' wouldn't have played a song over the phone on a dare.

"How about a game?" Becky said with a flip of her wavy black hair, trying to act tough and brave. She held out the basketball in her hands. It was a man's basketball, not a girl's size. She always hated whoever decided women weren't strong enough for a man's ball and had to create a women's ball instead. She was perfectly capable of doing whatever a man could do.

"Is this your way of asking me on a date?" the star of the Knights' basketball team asked with a boyish grin as he pointed to the ball she held out like a shield. "I think you had me already interested long before you called me last night."

"You liked me before I called you last night?" she asked in surprise.

"I didn't know it was you last night until I heard Andrea in the background, but yes, I liked you long before last night. I've liked you since the country fair and you ran away from me after our Ferris wheel ride like a demon was on your heels. I thought you hated me by how fast you sped away."

"I thought you didn't really like me and only felt sorry for me that night."

"No, I actually liked you. If I didn't like you, I wouldn't have followed you around all night from ride to ride and stood behind you in line just to get you to notice me. You turned me into a stalker at the young age of thirteen," he laughed.

"So, Carmen was right…" Becky murmured under her breath.

"What?"

"Nothing," she said quickly when she realized she had

uttered the words out loud.

He smiled and said, "I wanted to ask you out after you rode with me, but I couldn't because all that was in front of me was dust from you speeding away."

"Why didn't you ask me out over the past two years? It's not like we go to different schools or two years isn't enough time," Becky challenged with a touch of sarcasm.

"I'm a man. I wanted to ask you out many times after that day at the fair, but my ego wouldn't take the obvious 'no' I thought I'd get if I did," he surprised her by admitting.

"So, we wasted two years for nothing?" Becky summed it all up.

"Yep, but hey, we're only fifteen. Look at it this way, we still have many years ahead of us together..." He grinned, showing the huge craters in his cheeks. Damn, his dimples were gorgeous. She didn't need to go to the moon to see stupendous craters, for they were right in front of her.

"Cheesy line, but cute. Well... so, now what? We both like each other..." Becky said as she bounced the ball and switched hands easily from left to right and back again.

"I guess we play ball." He grinned and then added, "And for the record, I've seen all your games... you're darn good. I don't know if I have a chance to win in a game of one-on-one," He held up his hands in a defensive move. She looked into his bluish-green eyes, trying to decide if he was being sarcastic or if he was sincere. Becky decided he was actually being sincere.

"I've seen you play all your games, and you're good yourself. I think it'll come down to desire... and I don't like to lose," Becky said as she bounced the ball between her legs to the other side. "Game on!"

Two

It was strange how when she was fifteen her biggest challenge was taking a dare and calling the guy she had a crush on for two years, her biggest fear was meeting him on the basketball court to reveal her feelings. Now, that all seemed so silly and minuscule... not to mention a lifetime away.

The noise stopped. The silence jolted her back to reality. No more REO Speedwagon. Becky's heart began to beat faster again in the stillness.

"I'm right here. You're not alone. Just take a few soothing breaths and try to calm your breathing. I can hear you gulping air. Just remember you can only move your arms," the voice in her ears came back.

She didn't think she was going to make it through this. She was petrified but wasn't about to let him know how scared she was. She pictured a basketball in her hands and she was bouncing the ball. She bounced it left and then right. Right and then left. She focused on the imaginary ball.

Becky said in as calm a voice as possible, "I'm fine."

She wasn't about to admit to any weakness even though she was having trouble breathing. She was claustrophobic. Becky felt so stuck and so vulnerable—more vulnerable then she had ever felt in her entire life. She didn't think she was going to make it through the next set of pictures.

"Now, you're going to have two pictures in this next round and each one will be six minutes apiece approximately. There will be a pause in the middle of the pictures, so don't move thinking you're done. There'll only be a three second pause and not long enough to even move an arm or scratch an itch."

"I'm ready." She hoped she sounded better than she felt. She wished she could keep talking to him. His voice was so comforting—even more so than the music. However, she knew the longer she postponed the inevitable, the longer she would have to endure this procedure.

The machine started up again. The next song that came on was *'Nothing's Going To Stop Us Now'* by Starship.

Again her consciousness returned to the past, this time to her wedding day. The sand was cool beneath her bare feet. The sun was just setting over the horizon as Father Joe pronounced them man and wife. She was amazed how much the sunset looked liked her new husband's hair. It was red with a hint of yellow and maybe even in the right light, a little orange mixed in.

Seagulls were calling out in happy shrieks as they walked down the sandy path. Most brides had an aisle made of red carpet—she had a walkway made of seashells and beautiful golden sand. It couldn't have been a more perfect moment.

A huge white tent was waiting on the beach for their reception and the tables were set with white linens decorated with seashells and the most beautiful roses she had ever seen. The florist had said the flowers were called Tahitian Sunset Roses. They weren't in Tahiti, but she couldn't imagine it would be any prettier than what was before her now. She was soon going to find out though, for they were going to Tahiti for their honeymoon.

The orchestra played *'Nothing's Going To Stop Us Now'* as they walked through the opening of the tent to greet their waiting family and friends. Becky remembered taking her husband's hand and looking up into his cyan-colored eyes and smiling, their entire life stretching before them. She sighed with happiness and filled with contentment. The beauty of the roses didn't compare to her husband's eyes, the color reminding her of a dragonfly she'd once seen fluttering over a lake. Its body was kissed by shades of green and blue to create the same shimmering cyan color reflecting in her husband's eyes.

The noise stopped for a second… two… three… just like she was told. Then it started back up again. Becky felt hot tears prick her eyes with the memories of marrying her high school sweetheart who she fell head over heels for at thirteen.

She shouldn't cry. If she started to cry, it could mess up the pictures, which would mean longer in the confines of the machine or having to redo the pictures another day. The song switched to the classical notes of Mozart.

This walk down memory lane was killing her inside, but in an odd tortuous way, it also gave her something to focus on rather than the closing sensation in her throat. The image of her boys went through her mind as the music played. She remembered when she knelt on her knees praying to God for the stick to change colors and show a sign in the pregnant window. She wanted to be pregnant badly. She had lost four babies to miscarriages—which let such a pain in her heart she just couldn't explain to someone who hadn't gone through it. There were no words that depicted such a tragedy. However, the day she knelt on the floor, God had answered her prayers for the stick had yet again turned blue.

From the moment the pregnancy test proved she had life growing inside her, she stuck headphones on her stomach every second she could, piping classical music to her baby. Medical research was proving Mozart was good for a baby's developing brain. Oh, the brain, what a complex and important organ of the body.

She opened her eyes for a moment to look around. The soft tune still surrounded her, just like the halo machine. Except the halo around her own brain made her feel closed-in and helpless, and the music made her feel free. She quickly closed her eyes again and let the sweet melody envelope her, blocking out the reality. She tried to focus on the music, the sweet torturous music.

It's so odd how one event in one moment in time can change your entire perspective on life. God had thankfully blessed her with not just one baby, but two healthy babies. She had delivered twins.

She prayed so hard for the safe arrival of those children and over the years loved those children deeply... but... sometimes the work that went with that very blessing weighed heavily on her shoulders. The burden often made her angry and resentful at her husband for not helping more or sharing the responsibilities.

Even lately, now that the twins were older, she found herself grumbling about running them to this practice or to that game, the piles of dirty laundry and sweaty uniforms, and the sibling squabbles.

This moment in the MRI machine made her realize the very things she found herself resenting and complaining about were the very things that made her life whole and complete—the very things she had prayed to God for years that she wanted to be blessed with.

When had it become a chore? When, from the time the stick changed colors to the present moment in this doctor's clinic, had her perspective changed? What made her almost despise her husband for not helping more and the resentment of his freedom and carefree aura he put out when she had the care of her children pressing down on her? How and when had that changed? She hadn't realized it had until now. One day she prayed for the opportunity to change dirty diapers and fold and wash little clothes, to the next grumbling about those same piles of dirty clothes and the filthy toilets the boys couldn't hit properly.

However, lying here now, she felt like she'd wasted so much time harboring those negative feelings that she'd forgotten to enjoy every second and every dirty dish on the table, every toilet seat left up and every time laundry would be left on the floor.

There were so many occasions when she felt frustrated with life and the process of keeping up—the endless mountains of laundry, the constant demands of housework and her family and lack of help. Now, as she lay on the cool hard table, Becky wanted those days, months, those years back. She wanted to add them towards the future. The piles of dirty clothes and the muddy shoe marks on the floor, and even the fusses of not wanting to eat the dreaded green beans or broccoli, she wanted back... they no longer seemed like chores but blessings. She had regained the feeling she had before the pregnancy test. She had regained the feeling of being the luckiest woman alive to have two beautiful and healthy boys. It was like finding a twenty dollar bill in a pair of jeans you had hanging in your closet that you'd forgotten about, but a thousand times richer.

"Becky, you're doing just fine. Now, I'm going to have to take one of your arms out of the machine and give you a shot. It's just medicine that will allow the doctors to see your brain better," the voice came back again in her head. She waited and then she heard the door to her left ear open with a click and felt her arm being picked up and moved to the side. She felt fingers on her arm.

"I'll be done in a moment."

She wanted to scream to just get it over with. Every second in this box was agonizing, but she managed to say softly without moving her lips and jaw, "I'm ready when you are."

Becky felt her arm go back onto the pillow by her side and heard the door click shut. She heard the technician walk away, his soft-soled shoes scuffling lightly across the tiled floor. She couldn't turn her head to look at him and soon heard the same words all over again. The words that kept repeating in her head were 'hold still.' 'Don't flinch.' 'Don't move.'

She felt the swoosh of heat fill her body as the dye wound its way through her veins. It only lasted a minute but she felt a bead of sweat pop out on her upper lip.

"We're ready to take the rest of the pictures. You're halfway through now. Just try to relax and breathe deeply. I'm back at my station now and I'll give you instructions through the speakers in the machine. I'll be here with you the entire time. I'm not going anywhere... if you need me just talk to me. If there's an emergency, all you have to do is call for me," the voice told her. She was putting her faith in him.

"What kind of emergency?" Becky asked reluctantly. She was almost afraid to ask.

"Well... some people are so claustrophobic they hyperventilate and pass out. Others get so upset they have to use the restroom or throw up. Some are sick when they come for the test and have to be monitored closely for medical reasons."

"I see. Well, I felt perfectly fine coming in here today... except for my headaches and the occasional blurred vision in my right eye. I guess I shouldn't complain about any of this, it could be worse and according to you, sometimes is," Becky said and closed her eyes tight. "Bring it on."

"All right. Here we go again. Just think of the music

you're hearing as something to focus on, to take your mind off where you are. Mind over matter."

The trip down memory lane with the music wasn't easy, but the only other reason she was going to make it through this contraption any longer was the music. It was a double-edged sword.

"I can do this... I know I can. Just turn on my music nice and loud," Becky commanded and then remembered her manners. "Please."

She was tough. She could do this. She was a strong woman.

"Hang in there..." he soothed as the music filled in his sentence... *Beer for my horses...*

Toby Keith with Willie Nelson. She wondered if the people singing all the songs she was listening to knew how thankful she was for them and the songs they created. Did they know their music was her saving grace... her strength?

Becky's mind wandered again to her life. She was guilty as most people of taking things for granted. It never dawned on her she wouldn't have another day or another sunrise or sunset. The beauty of everything around her wasn't something she really noticed anymore. Everything was fast-paced and scheduled. How ironic the very MRI procedure she was having today was also a scheduled event. The question was, did she have a calendar left to schedule anything else in the upcoming days, months, or years?

What about soccer on Thursday? Baseball on Friday? That birthday party on Saturday? She scolded herself. Nothing was certain yet. This was just a test to see if anything was really wrong. She could be perfectly fine. Great, in fact.

Becky thought back over her thirty-four years and tears misted her eyes. Damn it! She couldn't cry, wouldn't cry. Crying meant sniffing... sniffing meant doing this blasted test all over again. Crying also meant hiccups and the same result, another forty-five minutes in the machine from hell. She thought a second, or was it a machine sent from heaven? It was meant to find something wrong and hopefully to catch it early enough to fix it. Maybe this MRI machine was a blessing. She tried to focus on a more positive outlook rather than the negative approach she was harboring.

The clanging magically stopped as if sensing her newfound approval of it. She heard a very peaceful, "Becky? How are you doing?"

"Peachy."

She heard a low chuckle. "Good. I'm glad to know you're fine and fruity."

"How much longer?" Becky demanded.

"Let me look at all the data and I'll come back and tell you if we have everything we need."

"All right," she said in a calm voice, a composed feeling she was faking.

In her head she started to pray all the prayers she learned in Catholic school, the prayers she'd memorized for religious studies just because she had to and because Sister Margaret Mary insisted. Those same prayers she'd memorized now became so much more. They became a lifeline. A life preserver. She hung on tight to those prayers and started to repeat them. *Our Father Who Art In Heaven...*

Life was so strange. Becky spent all of grade school wanting to grow up and be in high school. She spent all of high school wanting to grow up and go to college. All of college was spent wanting to be done so she could get a job in the real world... and then when she got a job in the real world, she spent the next years wanting a baby. Life was full of wanting the next day, not living in the day that was given you. *Hallowed Be Thy Name...*

"Becky?"

"Yes?"

"You're done. You can get up now, collect your things out of the locker, get dressed and go home."

"Thank you," Becky said as she watched the halo part of the machine move away from her face. She was free but free to do what and for how long? She made her way to the locker room and then when she was sure she was alone, she dropped to her knees and prayed… *Thy Kingdom Come… Thy Will Be Done…*

Becky sat in her folding chair with the camera up to her eye. Thursday was soccer game day. Justin was about to score a goal. She yelled, "Go, Justin!"

Her son kicked the soccer ball, sending it sailing into the right top part of the soccer goal just out of the reach of the goalie's hands.

"Score!" the crowd around her cheered.

She shot the picture just at the right time. Justin's foot was in the air and the ball was flying into the net. Perfect. She hadn't brought the camera to a game in a while. Sure, she remembered occasionally but with so many games over the years, the camera bag had been left behind more times than not. Memories not documented… if… if…

"So, how's Justin doing?" a voice from behind her asked.

She turned and answered, "He's doing great. He just scored a goal."

"I'm sorry I'm late. Work kept me longer than I anticipated."

"That's all right, Kenny," Becky heard herself saying. She usually hated when he was late to his kids' functions… despised it even. Now, it didn't really seem that important. "I got a great picture of the goal and I'll email it to you later."

Kenny's face showed his surprise but his voice didn't reflect his face when he said, "Thank you."

"Sit down." Becky gestured toward the empty space on the lawn next to her chair.

He raised one eyebrow and took out his folding chair, opening it up and placing it next to her, asking casually as if they were best friends, "How's work?"

"Fine. I'm trying to find some good management and staff to run things more often so I can free up some of my time..." Becky stopped in mid-sentence because Justin was running by with the soccer ball in his possession and she cheered at her son, "Go, Justin!"

Her son passed the ball perfectly to his teammate... his twin brother, Adam.

"Go, Adam! Score!" Becky yelled, "Way to go, Adam!"

"Way to go Adam and Justin!" Kenny shouted over the cheers of the crowd.

"They grew up fast, didn't they?" Becky acknowledged. "I remember when we used to laugh and call their soccer games 'herd ball' because every player on both teams would be in a big bunch and look like a herd of cattle as they moved from one side of the field to the other. They have learned so much since those days."

"You did a great job teaching them how to play soccer. You've been working with the boys since they were able to walk," Kenny admitted with a sad expression on his face. "I should've helped more."

"You've done a lot in the past three years to make up for time lost at the beginning. You're a good father," Becky said with sincerity and a kindness she normally didn't address to Kenny anymore.

It was the truth. Kenny was nowhere to be found in the beginning four years of Adam and Justin's life. He'd missed out on so much. Her husband not being around and taking part in the family was a huge factor in why they had their arguments and falling-outs.

"I might've become a better father over the past several years, but I've lost a lot of special moments and time when they were small that I can't get back," Kenny said softly.

Over the years, Becky and Kenny had drifted apart and all the things they'd seen in each other and liked at the beginning were things that seemed to be wedged in between them now. She hated when he used to go play basketball Tuesdays and Fridays, the only nights he got off early from work. By the time he got home late the other nights of the week, the kids were asleep and all the household chores were done.

She'd spent those years watching all of the dads in the neighborhood playing ball with their children after they got off work, while she played ball with her boys to make up for Kenny not being home. She was the father they never had around.

Now, it just didn't seem as big of a deal. She supposed what should've been most important was that he loved them. She supposed that should've been enough at the time. Becky had held on to that bitterness all of these years—even though he had changed. The anger kept them apart.

She smiled and said, "You love your boys and that's what counts. I guess I should've been more understanding of that."

"Becky…"

"No, don't say a word. What's done is done. We've been divorced for over three years now. It's forced us both to grow up and to do things that maybe we should've done when we were married. It's made you spend more time with the kids and not expect me to be home all the time," Becky said honestly. "And it has required me to give you more of a role in the kids' lives and trust you with them more. I wasn't that good about letting you take the lead when you were around. It was hard relinquishing control and giving you a part when I ran the show ninety-nine percent of the time because you were gone with work or playing sports."

"I now realize I was acting like a spoiled child. I left you home in the evenings while I played sports and did all kinds of things with the guys. Now, I'm getting too old to play that hard and I've wasted all that time. I still l…"

He was interrupted by Justin and Adam's cries as they

ran toward both of their parents and screamed together, "We won!"

Adam skidded to a stop right in front of Becky and ran a hand through his sweat-drenched red hair. "Did you see my goal?"

Becky nodded. "We sure did."

Justin came to an abrupt halt right behind his brother and looked over Adam's slightly taller shoulder. "Did you see my goal and assist?"

"We sure did," Kenny answered, echoing Becky as he stood up and gave Justin's coal black hair a rub.

"What are you doing here, Dad?" Justin asked as if now realizing his dad had been watching him play. "Usually, you don't pick us up until after the game on your nights to have us."

"I decided to try to rearrange my schedule so I could see your game... actually I'm going to attempt to do that more often," Kenny answered with a half smile. "I miss seeing you boys in action."

"Hey, since you're both here, can we go out for pizza to celebrate our win?" Adam asked with excitement.

"I don't know..." Becky hesitated. This was probably the first time they'd all been in the same place for more than a few seconds in passing. Usually, they only saw each other as they dropped off the kids from house-to-house or game-to-game. It was a game of avoidance that took skill and talent.

"I'm not sure..." Kenny said as he looked at her with questioning eyes.

Becky thought back over her MRI she just had yesterday and surprised herself by saying, "Sure, why not?"

If anything was wrong with her, she wanted to spend every minute she could with her boys and if that meant enduring some awkward moments with her ex-husband, then she would do that, too.

"Great!" Justin and Adam both chorused. They had a tendency to say things together quite often. Becky just chalked it up to a twin thing.

"Great," Kenny said with a similar grin and motioned with his left hand toward the parking lot. Both boys had his perfect smile.

A glitter caught her eye. Kenny still wore his wedding ring. The divorce had been final for three years and yet that gold band was still on his finger. Becky asked him about it once casually and he told her, 'It gives me peace from all the single women who are looking."

She didn't understand what red-blooded man wouldn't want to get right back out there and date. Becky had no doubt that women were probably knocking on his door and calling him day and night after their divorce. She'd imagine that to most women, Kenny was a perfect catch. He was kind, gentle, had such a great body with the cutest little mole... She was unable to finish her thought because of a sound of a clearing throat.

Becky's eyes widened at the sound and stared into his watching eyes, a deep blush staining her cheeks an attractive crimson. Thankfully, Kenny didn't say anything in front of the boys. She glanced down at her own left hand and the plain wedding band that matched her ex-husband's glistened up at her. She no longer wore the diamond, but had left on the band. Becky told herself it was to detour any men trying to pick her up, the same excuse Kenny was using. She told herself there wasn't time or energy to mess with dating, but now as her heart was fluttering, she was wondering if she was telling herself the truth.

"Whose car should we ride in?" Adam asked, looking from the white Volvo to the white truck. It was obvious she and Kenny both liked white.

Becky supposed they should ride with their dad because it was his time with the kids. "You can ride with your father. I'll follow."

"Why don't we all ride together?" Justin asked in confusion. "It'll save pollution."

"You're welcome to ride in my truck," Kenny offered, one eyebrow raised as if daring her to do it.

Her ex-husband was waiting for a reply. She coughed to cover her own unease and said, "No, that's all right, I'll just follow. I have to run a few errands down that direction anyway after we eat."

It wasn't a total lie. She did have to go pass the grocery store, but it just so happened that it worked as an excuse as well. They took separate cars. It was odd seeing that still. For years, Kenny, Adam, Justin and she would all go together in one car to games and out to eat. Now, however, they'd become what lots of divorced families have become, segregated and separated into my car and your car. My day and your day. My time and your time. She supposed there was nothing really wrong with that per say, but sometimes it became so much of what drove them that to be honest, it wasn't fair to the kids. Justin and Adam should be put first, not whose turn it was today.

A Catholic guilt-pain struck at her insides and she blew out a heavy sigh. Maybe she should've just gone with Kenny in his truck. But she didn't have a chance to change her mind and make up for the possible wrong choice about the cars. Kenny's truck had driven away.

Her white Volvo pulled up to the restaurant a short time later as Kenny and the kids were just getting out of the truck. He waited for her, which was something he hadn't done during their marriage.

She acknowledged his new thoughtfulness. "Thank you for waiting."

Kenny smiled and nodded. "You're welcome."

Justin and Adam piled into the booth first, leaving Becky sitting next to Kenny in the crowded little space. Her leg kept touching his every time she moved. She felt the spark of electricity between them just like when they were on the Ferris wheel ride but stronger because of their history together now. They never lacked for sexual chemistry what they lacked in other areas.

She found herself jumping each time their legs touched under the short table, bumping her knee against the bottom of the wooden slab.

"Ouch," she muttered after the last smack.

"Are you all right?" Kenny asked with what she thought was a mixture of a smirk and concern.

"I'm fine." It was her standard line.

Justin tapped her on the arm. "Mom?"

"Yes, honey?"

"Dad is taking us to the beach this summer. I believe to Watercolor. Why don't you come with us?" Justin asked innocently.

The soda Becky had in her mouth went flying all over the table and onto Kenny's arm. She tried to recover. "Umm.... sorry... the soda went down the wrong pipe." She cleared her throat before answering, "I...I...have to work. It's hard for me to get off for that long."

"But you're the boss. Can't you take off whenever you want?" Adam cornered her.

"Well, I guess technically I could but it's not that simple. I've been trying to find someone to run things for me when I'm gone." The minute the words were out, Becky almost choked again. This time it was from sadness of the double meaning of the word 'gone.'

Kenny noticed her discomfort and leaped to her defense. "What your mother's trying to say is, she's working on finding someone to take over some of her responsibilities at work so she can enjoy life a little more."

Becky gave her ex-husband a quick 'thank you' glance from under her long lashes and then added, "I'll try to come. That's all I can promise right now. Is that all right?"

"Yeah!" Justin clapped. He appeared for a moment younger than his seven years.

"All right!" Adam joined in on the applause.

"I said I'll try, I didn't promise to go," Becky clarified,

feeling like she'd just gotten suckered into a vacation with her ex-husband to the last place on Earth she wanted to vacation to right now.

Watercolor was where they had had gotten married. It seemed a lifetime ago and sadly she realized she might not have a lifetime in front of her anymore.

Becky coughed and managed to choke out in a whispered voice, "I think I need to use the bathroom."

Kenny slid out of the booth to let her scuttle past. He tried to touch her arm, but she moved away and made a beeline for the lady's restroom.

She heard him softly call, "Becky..."

She made it to the bathroom just moments before tears spilled down her cheeks. This was the first time she'd let herself cry since her chiropractor had told her she'd found a lump on the back of her head. Becky had gone to the chiropractor because she was having headaches and thought that stress, mixed with hunching over at work, had her neck and back out of sorts, but Dr. Rayen found a distension on her skull instead of tension. She recommended seeing her regular doctor for a second opinion. Becky remembered Dr. Rayen's eyes when she said seeking a second opinion was just a 'precautionary measure' and it could be 'just a harmless cyst.' The eyes always say more. Dr. Raven's eyes said so much more.

Becky had seen her primary doctor and he said usually everything was fine in situations like hers, but they would order an MRI just to be on the 'safe side.' The odds were supposedly 'in her favor' of everything being all right. However, she had a sinking feeling that those odds had failed her.

Becky slumped to the bathroom floor in despair. The old her wouldn't have dared to even place her purse on such a floor. The *her* sitting on the unsanitary tile just didn't care. Did a bacteria germ such as E. coli really matter at this point? Bring it on. She sobbed angry and sad tears all at once.

A gentle but firm arm went around her shoulders. She wasn't even concerned if she was making a fool of herself in front of some stranger in a public bathroom.

"Everything will be just fine… it'll be just fine. I'm here…" a familiar soothing voice murmured in her ear. It reminded her of a tone used to soothe fussy babies.

She couldn't stop the tears or the fact that her body was shaking uncontrollably. The pent-up emotions ruptured to the surface. Her boys' faces kept flooding her mind. She wanted to be around for them. She wanted to see them graduate high school, go to college, fall in love, get married, and then… she choked on the thought… her grandchildren.

"I'm right here. You're not alone."

Becky nodded with her head still in her arms. Her chin was gently lifted and she slowly raised her chocolate-colored eyes to meet bluish-green ones. A husky voice filled with emotion restated, "I'm right here. You're not alone."

But she *was* alone. She had no right depending on Kenny. He wasn't her husband anymore. She quickly jumped to her feet. It wasn't his job to take care of her. Besides, she didn't need taking care of. This was just a temporary break in her stone composure.

Becky sniffed and ran a hand across her face, clearing her cheeks of the salty mess of her tears. "I'm fine."

"Becky… talk to me…" Kenny said, placing his hand on her shoulder in a comforting gesture. The ring glittered on his left hand yet again in the cheap florescent lights of the bathroom.

She brushed his hand away. "I'm fine, Kenny, really I am." She took a deep breath and said matter-of-factly, "I can take care of myself."

"I don't know what to say."

"There's nothing to say. It is what it is. We're divorced. We have two children waiting for us to eat pizza, which by the way we should get back to since they shouldn't be sitting in a restaurant by themselves," Becky said quietly as she brushed a long strand of black hair off her athletic shoulders.

"I'm sorry for leaving them. I had to see if you were all right. The waitress said she would keep an eye on them," Kenny said, looking even more upset. "I want to help. We used to love each other… we used to…"

She interrupted Kenny's words. "Used to are the operative words. You have no obligation to care for me… and for the record, like I said before, I can take care of myself. I did for all of our marriage without much help from you." She couldn't resist throwing the last line in. She knew it wasn't nice to dredge up the past, but a small part of her was still a little bitter.

Becky turned sharply on her heel and walked back out the lady's bathroom door. A millisecond latter, she heard the hinges on the door creak again and a lady eating pizza next to her gasped loudly. It was a natural reaction to seeing a man coming out of the woman's bathroom. She almost had to smile as she wiped the tears from her eyes.

She heard the older voice say in a lecturing voice, "Men shouldn't be in the lady's bathroom."

She heard Kenny's answer, "Sorry, ma'am."

Adam and Justin were still sitting in the booth and were stuffing pepperoni pizza into their mouths.

Becky swallowed hard and did her best to act perfectly normal. "Hello, boys. How's the pizza?"

"Where were you and Dad?" Justin asked as Kenny walked up.

"We were… we were…" Becky faltered.

"We both had to go to the bathroom." Kenny shrugged, making it sound like they were in separate bathrooms.

"The pizza came and it was getting cold, so we decided to eat," Adam explained with a guilty expression on his face which went well with the pizza sauce on his left cheek.

Becky slid back into the dreaded booth and Kenny slipped in next to her. She banged her knee on the table a second time when Kenny's leg brushed against her own. Damn! She felt like she was a teenager all over again and they were on that Ferris wheel. Every time their legs had touched in that small metal carnival seat, she'd jumped and the seat would rock menacingly. Why did he have such an affect on her after all this time?

"I see I still make you jump," he whispered softly into her ear.

She pretended not to hear and struggled to pick up a slice of pizza. Justin and Adam talked the entire time about school and the game they'd just won. After about an hour, Becky stood up and said reluctantly, "I think I should go now." She gave both boys a kiss on the cheek.

"Maybe we can do this again sometime," Kenny ventured.

"Maybe," she called over her shoulder as she walked out of the pizza parlor.

Three

Kenny had the boys, but she tried never to miss a baseball game. Friday night baseball. Kids now-a-days were always so busy. Sports in her day used to go just for a few months, now every sport ran the entire year. You no longer had just fall soccer. Now you could play spring and summer soccer if you wanted, not to mention indoor soccer leagues for that snowy season. Baseball was the same way. It used to be spring and part of summer baseball, now it was played year round as well. She often told Justin and Adam to take a break, but they would beg to keep playing. At their age, they realized that if they didn't keep up with the sport, they would fall behind in skills and positions. Becky shook her head. It was a vicious cycle. She wanted the boys to be successful and happy, but at what cost?

"Justin's up to bat now," Carmen informed her.

Becky stopped daydreaming and paid attention to her son. He was batting third in the lineup. She asked Carmen, "Did I miss Blake batting?"

"Nope. He's batting fifth after Adam," Carmen replied, pointing to the batter's area where Adam and her son, Blake were warming up their swings.

"We're lucky to have such wonderful kids," Becky said with tears in her eyes. The tears frustrated her. It wasn't her usual nature to get this emotional.

Carmen noticed. "Are you okay, Bec?"

"I don't know," she admitted, "I honestly don't know." She glanced over at the crowd sitting behind the dugout.

"Are your test results back already?" Carmen asked with astonishment. Becky had told her friend that she was going in for the MRI.

Justin had a full count on him—three balls and two strikes. Becky waited for his swing and smack went the baseball.

Carmen yelled, "A double. He got a double!"

Becky had to smile at her friend's excitement. Her eyes automatically looked again at the crowd behind the dugout. Both of her sons were good at sports. However, she wanted them to realize there were more important things in life than sports. It took Kenny many years to realize what she figured out the minute she discovered she was pregnant. She wanted her boys to learn at an early age that sports had lots of great things about it, however, life had more wonderful things. Now Becky frowned. She didn't feel like she had gotten that message across as well as she should.

Adam hit a single and Blake hit a triple. Carmen was standing on her feet screaming and performing some kind of victory dance. "Way to go. Yeah!"

Carmen had that spunky personality. The kind of personality that was bubbly and bold. She was one of those friends that didn't care about what others thought about her or worried about speaking her mind. Carmen kept her brown tresses in a cute bob and her angelic face sprinkled with freckles tricked people into thinking she was docile and timid. She was nothing of the sort. She was a ball of spunk and fire.

"Shut your big mouth and sit your butt down so I can see my kid bat!" an irate man behind Carmen yelled.

Becky knew what was going to happen. She watched as her friend spun around and batted her lashes at the man sweetly and said, "Pardon me, sir. I guess your mother forgot to teach you how to speak to women. I'm surprised your wife has the patience to put up with you. Do you talk to her like that as well?"

His wife, who was sitting next to him, looked shocked for a moment and then glared at her husband. "She's right. You were rude. You shouldn't speak to women like that or anyone for that matter."

He opened his mouth to reply with obviously some smart comeback, but thought better of it since his wife's gaze grew even more menacing.

Carmen sat down in her chair like nothing happened. She went back to the subject Becky thought had been dropped. "So, your test results are back already?"

"Not really. I just have this gut feeling that the results are anything but good, that's all."

"How can you be sure you're right?" Carmen asked. "You're not a doctor, you know."

"I know I'm no doctor, but I know my body. I just know something isn't right."

"Maybe it's just paranoia. You shouldn't worry until there is need to worry," Carmen emphatically stated.

Becky really didn't want to talk about this matter, especially with people all around. She suggested, "Why don't we go get the kids a snow cone? I think the game's over and they look pretty thirsty."

"The game's over?" Carmen muttered, quickly turning around looking for Blake. Becky noticed her friend's eyes had locked on to something. She followed her gaze and sighed, then braced herself.

"Is that Kenny I see over there sitting behind the dugout?" Carmen pointed toward the crowed of spectators, and then said more loudly than Becky would've liked, "I never understood why you two don't at least sit together at your kids' games. It's obvious that you both want to. The entire time you're here, I catch you glancing to where he's sitting and he does the same for you. Such games are a waste of time if you ask me."

"I didn't ask you," Becky replied as she took her friend's shirt sleeve and gave it a tug in the direction of the concession stand. "The snow cone?"

"Fine. Let's go get a snow cone. But don't think that your little redirection worked on me. I'm just humoring you because I know you've been through a lot of stress lately and I'm taking pity on that fact."

They walked over to the little brown shack that was a makeshift refreshment stand. It was obvious somebody somewhere was trying to save money—probably to line their own pockets.

"I guess I'll see you tomorrow at Blake's birthday party," Carmen commented after giving the clerk their order.

"Actually, it's Kenny's time with the kids. He'll be the one to take them," Becky said as she took the cherry snow cones from the concession stand clerk. She did a double take. The girl had a tattoo on her arm of a cross. Even though it was sweet, she probably still had to be in high school.

Carmen noticed the tattoo as well and wasn't so quiet about it. "Nice tattoo. So, why did you decide to deface yourself at such a young age?"

The girl glared at Carmen and then finally said, "It's in memory of my dad. He died of a brain tumor last year."

Becky almost dropped the cones she was holding because her hands began shaking so badly. A stifling feeling came over her. She could hear her own heartbeat in her ears just like in the MRI machine. She knew she was going to lose it soon and turned, stumbling away from the crowd of people waiting in line for refreshments. Her eyes were starting to blur again. She swiped an angry hand across them like a windshield wiper on high.

She didn't know where she was heading, but she just knew she had to get away from the tattoo girl. It was a sign—a bad omen. Becky's legs wobbled and just before she was going to fall, she smacked into another body, like two pool table balls bouncing into each other.

"I'm so sorry. I wasn't watching where I was going," Becky apologized as her eyes traveled up to see who she rebounded off of.

It was Kenny. He was standing there with red cherry juice decorating his pleated tan work pants and light blue shirt.

"I'm so sorry," Becky apologized again, trying to dab at his shirt and then his pants. When she looked up, she couldn't help but marvel how blue his eyes seemed. It must be the shirt bringing out the blue tone, she thought. It amazed her how one minute they could look bluish-green and another, like now, the color of the sky on a clear day.

"No need to apologize." He leaned down and whispered in a husky voice, "But you might want to stop dabbing at my pants…"

Becky blushed profusely from his comment and quickly stood up, straightening her own shirt with a nervous hand. Carmen walked up, holding out new snow cones. "I got some extras since I saw the whole thing from over there… speaking of which you might want to get a room." Carmen shook her head and added, her eyes trained on Kenny, "Since you two obviously like each other still, I think you should tell Becky to come to Blake's birthday party tomorrow. He'd be crushed if Auntie Becky isn't there."

Kenny stared at Becky in surprise. "Why wouldn't you come to Blake's birthday party?"

"Well," she paused and continued, "It's your weekend with the boys."

"Carmen is your friend and you're Auntie Becky to Blake. You know he'll be heartbroken. Besides, I don't mind if you take the boys this weekend. We'll just rearrange the schedule," Kenny offered.

"No, I hate confusing them," Becky protested. "It took them a long time to get adjusted to the schedule they now have and the changes in their lives."

"Life shouldn't be a schedule, you know. You two need to just get back together and throw the schedule out the window," Carmen advised as only Carmen could do.

"Carmen," Becky growled in a low warning voice. She didn't want to get into it with her friend. They were best friends but that didn't stop them from disagreeing or arguing.

"If you won't get back together to solve this silly problem, then I have an idea. Why don't you both go? Imagine that. A simple solution to this dilemma," Carmen offered as she handed Kenny and Becky the snow cones. "Here. One for Adam and one for Justin."

"Thanks, Carmen." Kenny smiled and winked. "I always liked the way you think and the way you speak your mind. It's a great trait to have. People always know how and where they stand with you. You're probably a valuable commodity at your work."

"I like to be fair, exact and especially honest. Good communication is important to all relationships, work and otherwise. It's especially critical between two people in love. Maybe if you both communicated better, you wouldn't be standing here today like this—divorced."

Kenny nodded in agreement. "I believe you're right, Carmen."

Yeah, Becky knew exactly where Carmen stood—she wanted Kenny and her back together again. All of her friends, Andrea and Tammy Jane included, continually tried to talk her into working things out with Kenny. Heck, they were the reason she and Kenny met years ago on that Ferris wheel.

"So, guys, what do you say? Are you both going to my adorable son's birthday party?" Carmen gave a winning smile to close the negotiations.

"I don't know. I'm not sure that's such a great idea," Becky said in a worried voice. She remembered the other night at the pizza parlor. Regardless of the fact they were divorced, Kenny still had the ability to make her heart pound faster. She found it best over the past three years to avoid him for that reason. However, in light of the recent events, her guard was starting to slip.

"What would a few hours being together at a children's birthday party hurt? I think you're safe." Kenny gave her a cute boyish grin.

"I think she's chicken because she still has buried feelings for you and she can't trust herself to be around you," Carmen teased, one raised brown eyebrow daring her friend to deny it.

Becky flashed Carmen an aggravated look. "Sure, why not? It shouldn't be a problem since I have no romantic feelings whatsoever for my ex-husband anymore. We're just friends, that's all. Friends."

Carmen shook her head. "I believe you're trying to convince yourself more than you're trying to convince me."

"Carmen," Becky hissed in warning, ready to give her friend a piece of her mind.

Her pal was saved from her wrath by Justin running up to them. He gave Carmen a huge hug and a big happy grin. "Hi, Auntie Carmen."

"Hi, dear Justin. You played a great game. You and your brother both did." Carmen smiled down and patted his black hair. "You look more and more like your mother every day."

Justin grinned. "But I'm a boy."

"I mean your hair and how you talk. Of course, you're a boy, silly," Carmen admonished in a gentle voice.

"Is that snow cone mine?" Justin asked his dad, turning his attention to other matters.

"Yep, all yours." Kenny held out the treat.

"Why didn't you sit next to Mom like you did last night, Dad?" Justin asked innocently.

Becky noticed Carmen lean in, intrigued by this new bit of information. She was sure Carmen would now be even more adamant about playing matchmaker, knowing they'd been together so familiarly. Her friend would see an opportunity and would seize it—just like the Ferris wheel. It always came back to the Ferris wheel. Life felt like the same circle as that dreaded carnival ride.

"I work late one night, miss one game and obviously lots of good stuff," Carmen mused, looking from Kenny to Becky and back again.

Becky answered her son's question directed at Kenny. "I was sitting next to Auntie Carmen at this game and there was no more room."

"Yeah, bud. I had to sit on the other side of the field where there were seats. You had lots of fans today," Kenny covered.

The truth was, Becky probably could've made room if she'd scooted over more, but she wasn't sure she wanted to sit next to Kenny again. That blasted MRI brought out all the old memories and sappy feelings she had for him which were insane since they were divorced. And to make it even more insane, she was the one who'd wanted the divorce in the first place.

"Is that one mine?" Adam jumped up and landed on his father's back from behind. He was pointing to the cone in Becky's hand.

"Yeah, it is." Becky handed it to Adam when he jumped back to the ground and landed on his feet. She teased, "I see you're practicing for the circus."

"How about going out for dinner again with us, Mom?" Adam asked. "It was like old times last night at the pizza parlor."

"I'm sorry, honey. I can't tonight. I'll have to take a rain check," Becky said apologetically to her son.

Carmen studied them for a moment. "Interesting. You both sat next to each other at the game last night and you all went out to pizza together."

Becky knew what Carmen was thinking. She had to put an end to her matchmaking scheme that was already spinning in her head. "It was just a last minute thing. No big deal. Well, I need to get going. I'll see you boys next Thursday. I'll pick you up after the soccer game."

"No, you'll see them tomorrow at Blake's party," Carmen reminded Becky with a firm tone.

Becky was hoping to leave before she was dragged into a promise she didn't want to make. Obviously she wasn't going to with Carmen standing guard.

Blake came running up with his mitt in his hands. "Snow cones!"

"Hi, Blake," Becky greeted and walked over to give both her boys a quick hug goodbye and give Blake one as well. "I'll see you all soon."

"You'll see them all tomorrow at Blake's birthday party," Carmen grinned mischievously.

Blake happily jumped up and down. "Cool. I'm so glad you can come, Auntie Becky,"

"Fine, you'll see me tomorrow. Bye." She nodded toward Kenny and again gave her friend a nasty scowl.

Becky showed up to Blake's birthday party on Saturday wearing a cute little red dress. She greeted Carmen and gave her a quick hug and a kiss on the cheek. "Hi, sweetheart. How's the party going?"

"Don't 'hi' me. You look absolutely stunning in that little number. Are you hoping to impress a certain ex-husband?" Carmen jabbed Becky sharply in the ribs with her elbow.

"I don't know what you're talking about. I've always

thought you had an overactive imagination. I think it became worse after you went to college and got your Masters in marketing and business. They programmed you to have an even more creative and overactive imagination. I guess you chose your profession well." Becky proclaimed, trying to redirect her friend off the subject of Kenny and her red dress.

"Kenny and the boys are already here and sitting out back by the pool. I hope you have your swimsuit under that sexy little number," Carmen remarked with a wink.

"I do, but I doubt if I'm going to swim," Becky informed her as she walked in the direction of the backyard.

"Give Kenny a kiss from me, would ya?" Carmen yelled after her. Becky swore she heard her friend snicker.

She kept walking. Becky found Kenny lounging in a lawn chair looking charmingly delectable. Even after all this time, he still had a great body. His calves were muscled and well-shaped like Superman's calves, rock solid from years of training and playing basketball. When they were in high school, she'd watched as he practiced. The team would start on the baseline of the basketball court, run to the first line on the court and then run backwards to the baseline. The team had to do that maneuver for every line on the court and keep repeating that drill until everyone on the team felt sick.

"Hi, Bec." Kenny smiled and stood up immediately when he saw her.

"Hi, Kenny. How are the kids?"

"They're great. After the game last night we rented some movies and had 'Movie Night' with popcorn smothered in butter," Kenny told her.

She felt a pang of jealousy. She wanted to be there with her boys watching movies and eating fattening popcorn. Instead, she'd gone home and researched tumors on the Internet. Becky hated missing out on moments with her children… moments she might not have in the future.

"It sounds like you had a great time. I'm sorry I wasn't

there." She found she actually meant it.

"Really?" Kenny asked, surprised at her confession.

"Yes. I hate missing things like that with the boys. I really wish I could've been there. I love buttered popcorn. I miss those things."

"And me? Do you miss me?" Kenny's eyes grew serious and for a moment he looked like a man rather than the boy she always thought him to be and even acted like most of the time. Although, since the divorce, she must admit there was a new side to him she'd never seen before. She wasn't sure if that side had always been there and she hadn't taken the time or even wanted to see it, or if the side was the direct result of the divorce.

She decided to tell the truth and give him an honest answer. "And you."

Kenny took a step closer and as he spoke, his soft voice washed over her. She could feel her knees start to wobble. "Becky, I've missed you so much over these…"

"Becky!" Andrea came bounding over and threw herself in between them and hugged her best friend. "I was hoping you'd be here."

Becky cleared her throat, struggling to gain composure. "Hi, Andrea. Where's Chloe?"

"Oh, she's hanging with all the boys which has her mother very nervous." Andrea pointed toward a beautiful blonde girl. Andrea's daughter, Chloe, was only six but she towered above all the kids her age. She looked like she was nine.

"Andrea, I don't know how you do it having a girl. I think I'd lock her in a closet until she was thirty." Kenny shook his head over the prospect of having to deal with a daughter and boys who admired her.

"It isn't easy, that's why I have her in Tae Kwon Do. When she's of dating age, she can kick butt if she wants to. She's already a first degree black belt," Andrea informed them proudly.

Andrea herself barely stood five-foot two, but her husband was six-foot six. It always amazed Becky how two totally different people could hook up and fall in love. Becky frowned as her thoughts drifted toward the couple. She never thought Andrea and her husband would stay together, but every time she saw them, they looked like two lovesick puppies. Yet, she and Kenny, who had so much more in common, were divorced. Go figure that one, she told herself.

"Why the frown, dear friend?" Andrea asked as she flipped her blonde ponytail to her back in cheerleader fashion. Andrea had been one heck of a cheerleader growing up and because of her size, made a great top to the pyramid for the squad.

"Nothing. I'm just getting a little hungry that's all," Becky said, glancing toward the barbecue grill. "The hot dogs and hamburgers smell great."

"Why don't you chat with Andrea and I'll grab you something to eat?" Kenny offered.

Kenny had never been one to offer anything when they'd been married so his suggestion gave Becky a start. The married Kenny would never offer to get her something to eat. He was selfish and would've gotten something for himself instead. During moments like this, she wished the divorce had never happened.

"Um, that would be great, thanks. I'll take a hot dog with…" Becky didn't get a chance to finish.

"Dill pickles. I remember." Kenny smiled and headed off toward the food table.

"I never understood the pickles, relish maybe, but dill pickles? Yuck." Andrea's nose wrinkled in distaste, and then she waved her French manicured finger at Becky. "Speaking of not understanding something, I don't know why you divorced Kenny anyway. He's a great guy. We all think so. It's just sad you stopped seeing that."

"It's complicated."

She watched Kenny walk away and noticed a hot-looking blonde with big breasts popping out of her leopard-print bikini watching him as well. The woman definitely stood out, not only from her chest size, but also in looks. There was no doubt how gorgeous she was. And Becky knew her. The woman was recently divorced as well. Andrea had told her the woman's husband had left her because he found her in bed with another man. Lots of women, especially the desperate type, would kill for a man like Kenny.

Four

"What's so complicated about it? You two loved each other back then, you love each other now and you'll love each other five years from now. That doesn't sound so complicated to me," Andrea lectured her friend.

"It is complicated," Becky repeated.

"I think you've made it more complicated than it really is. Your boys need both of their parents around and what if…" Andrea cut off her words before she said them.

Andrea also knew of her MRI. Becky never kept anything from her friends. However, she was starting to wonder if she'd made the right choice telling them so soon. She should've waited until after she really knew if there was a reason to say anything. "What if I die? Was that what you were going to say?" Becky asked point blank.

"I shouldn't think like that. I'm sorry."

"No, you're right. What if I do die? There's always that chance. There's always a chance, for all of us, that we won't have tomorrow. Mine just seems a little more real because of the situation, but any one of us can die tomorrow. Car accident. Heart attack. Any type of accident. It's possible," Becky said, waving a hand in the air. "It's possible, but it just seems more possible for me, doesn't it? Is that the point you're trying to make?"

"Becky, I didn't mean to be negative. Every minute you have with your children is so precious. Those memories mean so much to them. Memories with their mother. I don't want you to waste any of those minutes to make memories with Justin and Adam." Andrea hesitated and then added, "And with Kenny. He's the man you love and you're stupid for not getting back together when you need him most."

Becky's jaw dropped open. "You're lucky that I outgrew the stage of putting you on silent probation like when we were in school."

"Go ahead. You know it needed to be said," Andrea dared as only a friend could. She was starting to sound as bold as Carmen, Becky thought, which wasn't like Andrea at all. She was the sweet sensitive one.

"Even if, for argument's sake, I did want to get back with Kenny, that I still loved him, I wouldn't want to now anyway. I don't want us to get back together because I might have a tumor and could be dying."

"You *are not* dying. The woman standing before me looks hot and healthy and it wouldn't be out of pity if he knew about your condition. He still wears his wedding ring, for goodness sakes!" Andrea's voice rose. Becky could always hear her friend's voice over any crowd. She attributed it to cheerleading training.

"Keep your voice down," Becky shushed, "Why don't we just drop the subject?"

"Drop what subject?" Kenny asked as he walked up holding three hot dogs. "I got one for you too, Andrea."

Becky hoped that Andrea wouldn't tell him what they'd been discussing. At this moment, she was uncertain if Andrea would or not. Her friend was clearly passionate about this topic.

"You're so sweet," Andrea gushed and then gave Becky one of those 'I told you so looks' and continued,

"We were just talking about girly things, and you know how boring that can be to a man."

Becky didn't say anything. She just took the hot dog with dill pickles. "Thank you."

"Well, I'm going to check on Chloe. She just got into the pool and I need to keep an eye on her."

"Bye, Andrea," Kenny said and gave her a kiss on the cheek.

"Bye, Andrea." Becky gave her friend a hug. Andrea nodded, knowing that all was forgiven between friends. The hug said everything.

"It wasn't about girly things, was it?" Kenny said after Andrea had gone.

"No. I really don't want to talk about it right now. I just want to enjoy the party and our boys. Speaking of which, where are they?" Becky asked looking around.

"They're shooting hoops around back. Do you want to go check on them?"

"Sure, I always feel better keeping an eye on them," Becky admitted. She was like Andrea in that respect. Kids could get into mischief so quickly.

"I remember when you used to creep into their nursery all the time when they were sleeping and check to make sure they were still breathing," Kenny smiled fondly.

"I couldn't help it. Once a mother, always a mother." Becky smiled back, forgetting for a moment about her health. "Let's go find the boys."

They found Justin and Adam shooting baskets with a bunch of their friends and their dads. Justin held the ball in one hand and motioned them over. "Come on. Join us for a pick up game."

Kenny glanced at Becky as if asking permission. He was looking at the basketball with such love and longing. It was then she realized she'd tamed him over the years and now felt horrible. Maybe in a crazy way she was jealous of the basketball.

She used to get so upset when he played basketball after they had kids, but ironically the very thing that made her fall in love with him at the beginning, was now the very thing she resented. By resenting basketball, she was in reality resenting a part of him, a part of him that she'd loved. Becky was starting to understand everything now, years too late.

He shouldn't have to come to her for permission for something as trivial as playing basketball with his kids—especially since they were now divorced. She blinked away the tears and said, "Go on and make your boys proud."

His face lit up with excitement as he ran towards them with the gait of a happy kid. He looked free. She had caged him and now she had set him free.

Adam looked over at his mother. "Now we're uneven for teams. You'll have to join us, Mom."

Becky shook her head. "I don't think so. I'm not exactly dressed for the sport." She was in a red slip dress overtop of a red bikini swimsuit. Not exactly dressed out to play sports.

"Take off your sandals and play bare-footed. That's what we did." Justin pointed to his own bare feet. His innocence didn't grasp the fact that she had on a dress and a bikini top that didn't give her full figure nearly enough support for jumping around and shooting a basketball.

"It's a man's ball, the kind you tell stories about liking to play with," Justin pointed out, tossing her the ball. She couldn't tell if he was knowingly teasing her or not. Did he sense his mother's buried love for basketball? The love she buried because she put herself last for so long?

"That's my old life. I haven't touched a ball since, well, since before you were born," Becky told Justin with a grin.

Still, she held onto the ball, the itch to shoot too strong to let go. It felt similar to when she'd given up caffeine. When she smelled a cup of coffee brewing or picked up a coffee mug, the need to have a cup was almost enough to drive her running into the break room at work and gulping down the entire pot. She could hardly contain her addiction to run down that court and shoot the ball through the hoop.

"Come on, Becky. Like the old days." Kenny moved his arms in a defensive position like he did that day when she'd met him on the basketball court and they'd played one-on-one in the high school gymnasium.

It was just too tempting. The desire to play basketball ran much deeper in her core than the desire for caffeine. She was an addict that had suppressed her addiction for too long. Becky succumbed.

She grinned, now knowing why Kenny seemed so happy and free a minute ago. "Game on. Let's play ball!"

Playing basketball was almost like a fever, the desire to play was hard to contain once you fell in love with it. She kicked off her shoes and shot the ball. Swish, right into the net, just like the old days.

"The game hasn't started yet. Those two points don't count! We still need to redo teams and start a new game to be fair," Justin protested the point.

Adam grinned. "Justin, for the record, it was a three point shot and I'm on Mom's team."

"I'm on Dad's team then," Justin said, giving Adam a teasing look that only a brother could do.

The rest of the players were chosen and the game began. Becky didn't miss the fact that Kenny watched her every move. His eyes seemed to be focused on her lack of a support bra.

She finally jabbed him in the ribs in a defense move and hissed, "Eyes up!"

Kenny had the decency to blush as he swung around, avoiding her guarding arms to shoot the ball. He scored. She groaned. She hated to be outmaneuvered.

He walked by her and whispered, "I think every man on this court has noticed not only that you're excellent at basketball, but you're gorgeous as well."

Becky rolled her eyes as she took the basketball to pass it in. She threw it to Adam, cut around Kenny and then performed a quick move to get open. Adam threw it back to her and she did a lay-up to score.

"We're ahead!" Adam bragged, doing a victory dance.

"Not for long," Justin told his twin brother with a wrinkling of his nose. Justin had his mother's competitive nature.

The game went on for an hour. Becky had beads of sweat dripping down her face, her body drenched in perspiration. But regardless of that fact, she felt so alive. It had been a long time since she'd played like this. She thought she had to give it up for her children, but looking around the court at her boys, she now understood she didn't have to give up what she loved. Becky realized how wrong she'd been about a lot of things when it came to motherhood. Sure, there were sacrifices to make, but she could still be herself. She didn't have to give up who she was to be a mother. There was obviously a way to do both. Today, on this court, was proof of that.

"Game point," Kenny called.

Becky shifted to the left, then back to the right and spun around Kenny just like he'd done to her earlier. However, instead of scoring herself, she passed to Adam. Her son shot the ball and everyone stopped to watch the ball roll around and around the outer rim. There was complete silence. Becky and Kenny looked at each other. Then the ball fell into the net.

"I won the game!" Adam shouted in victory.

Kenny picked Adam up and put him on his shoulder. "You sure did, son."

Becky cheered and the entire court shouted in approval. Adam looked at his dad with loving eyes and said, "You're on the other team. You shouldn't be cheering for me."

"I'll always cheer for both my boys," Kenny replied in a loving tone.

Becky looked at her family and for a second wished they were all together again.

Kenny set Adam down. "Let's go cool off in the pool."

"Yeah!" Justin squealed, obviously liking the idea.

Everyone ran off in the direction of the pool. Kenny was holding the boys' hands and following the crowd. Justin and Adam were telling him something and it must've been funny, because Kenny was laughing.

She looked on in despair. Becky felt like a person watching a movie play out before her eyes. She wanted to be in the scene, but didn't quite know how. It felt so surreal. She felt like she was looking down on her life and what it would be like without her in it. Kenny and the boys together without her.

Becky was still watching when Kenny paused and turned around. His eyes met hers and he asked with a smile, "Are you joining us?"

She wanted to go along for the journey with them. She truly did. Adam and Justin both had huge welcoming smiles on their faces. Their love broke through that feeling of being on the outside looking in. Becky nodded and ran to catch up. Justin took her hand and off they went together toward the pool. They looked like preschoolers all holding hands to stay together. Becky held on tight. She didn't want to get left behind.

When they arrived back at the pool area, Justin and Adam both jumped in doing simultaneous cannon balls, making a huge water geyser that shot into the air. The water hit Becky's legs and was an icy cold reality slap. It just dawned on her that they were actually going swimming. The realism of Kenny seeing her in a swimsuit hit her like that cold water.

She supposed a small part of her wanted him to see her, otherwise she would've worn her ugly checkered one-piece swimsuit instead of the bright candy apple red two-piece. The mischievous and devilish side had won while she was getting dressed.

Now she wished the angel side had won as she slowly slipped off the sweat-soaked red dress. She gulped and removed it completely. Becky looked around and saw Kenny staring at her with eyes blazing with an all too-familiar desire. She wanted to throw her dress back on, but she didn't want Kenny to know she was affected by any of this. It shouldn't matter if she didn't like his attention anymore… right? Becky eased into the water and shivered.

Kenny came over and put his arm around her. "Warmer?"

The breath she must've been holding hissed out of her lungs, sounding like a balloon someone pricked with a needle to let the air out. She shivered again. This time she knew it wasn't from the cold water, but from being in Kenny's embrace.

"Becky?" Kenny said in a gravelly voice close to her ear.

"Kenny, this probably isn't such a good idea…"

"I don't think there's ever been a better idea."

"If you took a step back, you'd realize it's nothing more than forgotten memories stirred up. If we did what I can tell you're thinking, we'd be back to fighting and miserable after the newness wore off or until I…" Becky couldn't quite say the word 'die.'

"It's not like that. What I feel isn't newness. I never stopped loving you… *you* stopped loving me. You were the one who wanted the divorce, not me. I wanted to try to work it out," Kenny said, nearly bordering on anger now.

"See, it's starting again… the anger toward each other."

"No, what's starting is the anger I feel toward you

leaving me because of 'irreconcilable differences', according to your overpaid lawyer," Kenny replied, the muscle in this jawbone twitching. Becky pushed him away and tried to put distance between them. She was able to make it two steps.

"I left you because you always put us last behind work, playing basketball, playing baseball, and even watching sports. You were never romantic. We always argued over everything... like you not helping with the dishes, laundry or housework or even your own kids. Bottom line, we always argued."

"I've changed since the divorce," Kenny defended himself. He moved one step closer to her.

"You shouldn't have to change. We should've loved each other for who we were. I shouldn't have wanted to change you. I should've been all right with who you were."

"That's not true. You had the right to expect me to help out around the house, especially since we both worked. I guess I always figured since it was your pharmaceutical companies that you had an option to work or not to work, so my work came first. I know that wasn't true now," Kenny said sadly. "I was pigheaded and wanted to be the main provider. The one who made the most money. We were supposed to be a team. I shouldn't have looked at it the way I did. I wanted to be the superstar and I wanted you to be on the bench cheering for me. I wanted to force you into a role that I knew wasn't who you were. You were always the one who wanted in the game."

"Kenny, we can't do this. We know why we got divorced. It's been over three years now. You've moved on and I've moved on. Whatever the reasons for the divorce, what we had is in the past." She took one more step away. They seemed to be doing a dance in the water—two steps away ... one step closer ... one step farther...

"No, Becky, we're standing here right now in the present—not the past as you can see—and we're both still wearing our wedding rings. There has to be something worth trying to save." Kenny took a half step toward her.

"So, maybe we both grew up and changed some, but that doesn't mean we could work out our problems. It would be too confusing for our children if we tried it again and we failed again. It's not fair to Adam and Justin emotionally for us to screw up a second time. We owe it to them not to do this." Feeling vulnerable, Becky tugged at her bikini top trying to cover more of herself.

"I think just the opposite. I think we owe it to the boys and ourselves to try." Kenny's gaze watched her attempts to fix her slipping top.

He moved through the water closing the distance. He now stood toe to toe with her. The dance had ended. Kenny took the strap behind her neck that she was trying to retie in his hands and leaned over her to secure the ends. The top of her body was pressed against his. When she inhaled, memories flooded over her. He seemed to be tying awfully slowly. When she felt the bow pull tight, she pushed at his smooth chest and backed away from him. The dance began again.

"Thanks for helping with my swimsuit. I think it wiggled loose during our game of basketball," Becky admitted breathlessly.

He moved closer still. "You're welcome." Kenny took his hand and lifted her chin so she was gazing up into his handsome face. "Becky, we're meant to be together, it's that simple. Stop trying to complicate everything. Sure, no matter what we'll always have problems, that's part of being married. You need to focus on the positive things and what we did... What we do have."

"It's too late for many reasons." Becky inhaled and quickly dove under the water and swam to the other end of the pool. Dance over. The band went home. She had to get as far away from him as possible. Unfortunately, forty feet wasn't that far. Her heart was still beating as fast as the wings of a hummingbird. Everything was different now. If only they would've had this conversation one year, two year or even three years ago. If only she would've realized how she had made mountains out of little things. If only she would've turned what she thought were negative things into positive things. If only... so many of those.

Andrea and Carmen both swam over to where she stood. Carmen spoke with her normal bold spirit. "Why don't you two just bury the past and get on with your future? I was afraid all the people in the pool would get electrocuted from the electricity you both were putting off over there. We all see it. Why are you so blind?"

"I'm not blind. Kenny and I have always had chemistry, but it's the other things we have trouble with," Becky defended herself.

"What else is there besides chemistry?" Carmen inquired, shocked. "In my book that's all you need."

"Oh, pish-posh. You know there's more to marriage than chemistry, and for the record you both have it. Don't you remember for better or worse when you got married?" Andrea stated.

"I thought those were just words," Carmen grinned.

"Don't be silly. They're not just words. You're supposed to be together through the bad times and the good—through sickness and health until..." Andrea stopped short yet again. "I'm so sorry, Becky. Me and my big mouth."

"Don't be sorry. It could be true if we were still married, but we're not. What you're saying no longer applies to us and Kenny doesn't owe me through sickness and health until death do us part. It's not his place or his job anymore. Maybe this divorce was a good thing. He's grown up and has taken a much more active role in the children's lives. I don't think he would've been ready like he is now to take over if... well... if anything does happen to me," Becky said as she wiped a tear from her cheek. "Water in my eyes."

"Stop being so negative for goodness sake, girl. Your

own doctor hasn't even called you yet with the 'bad' news you think you're going to get. You could be wrong. Everything could be just fine. We all need to stop thinking like you're sick and could die. Even if you had a brain tumor, it doesn't mean you're going to die. Geez, girlfriends, let's get out of this pity party hole and think positive." Andrea rooted like a great cheerleader. "I, for one, am deciding right here and now to be more positive."

"Yeah, you go girl! We're all way too negative. Why don't we get out of this blasted cold water and go get a glass of wine?" Carmen suggested.

"Sounds good," Andrea agreed, wiping water out of her own eyes as well.

Becky smiled and said, "I'd like that."

As they were getting out of the pool, Becky noticed the woman wearing the leopard bikini flirting with Kenny. She couldn't help the jealousy in the pit of her stomach or the desire to go over there and put the bimbo in her place. Then she realized she was the one who was out of place. Kenny wasn't her man anymore. That woman had all the rights and she, Becky, was the one who had none.

Kenny came on over with the boys a while later. Becky, Carmen and Andrea were sitting on lawn chairs sipping wine. She made sure the lawn chairs were facing away from the pool and the leopard print lady.

Her ex-husband yawned as he addressed Carmen, "I think the boys and I are heading home. All of your guests are gone besides us and it's getting late."

Becky glanced at her cell phone checking the time and agreed, "It's later than I thought. I guess I should be leaving as well."

"Why don't you stay? I've got the boys anyway. Stay and visit with your friends," Kenny said as he wrapped a towel around Adam and then Justin's shoulders.

Carmen agreed, "Yeah, stay."

Andrea smiled. "Let's have a slumber party like old times. What do you girls say? Shall we act like teenagers again… without the acne?"

"I don't have any clothes with me," Becky protested.

Carmen urged, "Come on. Live a little. I'll find something for you to wear."

"We're too old for slumber parties," Becky reasoned.

"You're never too old for slumber parties." Carmen grinned as she took a sip of her wine.

"I think you've had enough to drink. You're getting too tipsy to think straight," Becky teased her friend.

"I'm fine. I just think it'll be fun." Carmen sat her glass down before she spoke. "Sometimes you have to live in the moment."

"Let's do it," Andrea encouraged.

Kenny slipped off the dark green tee shirt he was wearing. "You can sleep in this if you want."

Becky couldn't move her arms. Carmen took it out of Kenny's hands and threw the shirt on her lap. "That takes care of jammies for Becky. Who says a man wouldn't give the shirt off his back for the woman he loves?"

Andrea's husband walked over and caught part of the conversation. "What's this about a man giving a shirt off his back for the woman he loves?"

Andrea gave her husband a loving look. "We're staying at Carmen's house for a sleepover and we're trying to find some clothes for bedtime."

He leaned down and kissed the top of his wife's head and then took off his shirt. "Anything for you, babe."

Andrea giggled at her husband. "But, I'll look like a drowned rat in your shirt."

It was Carmen's turn to giggle. "We can pretend it's a wedding dress with a big long train."

Carmen and Andrea laughed hysterically. Becky on the

other hand couldn't help but think of weddings and, of course, Kenny.

"I guess we'll see you on Thursday." Kenny shifted his feet uncomfortably. Becky wondered if he was thinking the same thing she was.

"How about seeing Mom tomorrow? Can you come with us to church in the morning, Mom?" Justin pleaded.

It was like her son sensed something between his parents and was trying hard to piece it together. Justin and Adam had stopped trying to get them together after the first year of the divorce. Why all of a sudden were they starting now? Was it that obvious that something was brewing under the surface... even to seven-year olds?

"Come on, Mom," Adam pressed when Justin elbowed him in the ribs. "It's just church."

It was hard to turn down an invitation to church, especially in light of the current situation. She nodded. "I can meet you at church this Sunday. Just save me a spot in the pew."

Justin and Adam giggled at the word 'pew' and Kenny gave them a firm but gentle look. "Boys, show some respect for God." They quickly sobered and swallowed their giggles.

Becky walked over and gave the boys a kiss. "Have fun with your dad."

It was going to be hard to go to church with Kenny again. They went to the same church still, but on different days. She went on Saturday nights and he went on Sunday mornings. This schedule had worked for three years and now it was going to be breached. Now she was wondering if that was wise.

With a hand on each of their shoulders, Kenny guided the boys in the direction of their car. "Have fun on your sleepover," he called to her.

Becky just nodded. His shirt still in her hands.

Five

The priest stood outside the doors greeting the congregation. She shook his outstretched hand.

"It's good to see you at Sunday morning church, Becky. Your family, where God wants you to belong, is in the first pew."

Becky managed to say, "Thank you, Father Joe."

Father Joe wasn't so happy when she and Kenny had split up. He'd tried for three months to get them back together with counseling and guilt. She had wanted no part in reconciling their marriage and just went through the motions for Father Joe's sake. It was hard to say 'no' to a man of God when you'd known him since your baptism. The counseling hadn't worked. Yet, here was Father Joe still trying. She had to give him credit for perseverance. He was a good leader of a wonderful church. Becky glanced around the chapel.

The church stood open and beautiful before her eyes. It was strange how she never really noticed it until today. The cross with Jesus hung from the enormous vaulted ceiling and overshadowed the entire place. Overcome, tears welled up in her eyes. She believed in God. She was raised to believe in God, but it was more out of routine than something in her soul. When she walked into church today, her soul tingled. It was that tingling that scared her the most. Was God calling her home?

Kenny waved. Justin and Adam had huge smiles on their faces. Becky eased into the pew next to her boys on the end. Justin gave her cheek a kiss. "Hi, Mom."

"Hi, Justin. You look nice in your suit. Your father did a good job of dressing you."

It was strange how much had changed over the years. When they were married, Kenny never really helped with the boys' care, but they sat before her today completely and very handsomely groomed by their dad.

"Hi, Mom." Adam leaned over and kissed the same cheek.

"You both look very nice today," Becky complimented and turned to address Kenny. "You did a good job of getting them ready."

"Thank you," he answered quietly.

He always seemed shocked at her compliments. She supposed in his defense, when they were married, she always found fault with what he did or didn't do. Maybe space and age had given her perspective just as it seemed to have given him grooming skills.

The church organ started to play and Father Joe walked up the aisle holding his trusty Bible reverently in his hands. He nodded to the boys and all of a sudden Justin and Adam stood up and walked in front of her and sat down on her right side.

She whispered to them, "Boys, go back to where you were..."

Father Joe shuffled his feet by her pew and gave her such a stern look, she squirmed. She felt like she had when she'd gotten in trouble for talking during church from Sister Margaret Mary. Father nodded his satisfaction and then continued on to the altar. Becky glanced over at Kenny who was now sitting two empty spaces from her on the left. He looked so isolated, it hurt.

Her heart skipped a beat at the thought of what she should do to be polite. She slid down closer to Kenny. The boys, upon seeing her move over, scooted closer to her. Justin and Adam both had happy smiles on their faces. They were good... very good. Even better than Carmen, Andrea and Tammy Jane all those years ago when they did the old switcheroo on the Ferris wheel ride. Becky supposed her boys had Divine help in the matter. She took a moment and studied Father Joe. He was pretty sneaky for a man of the cloth. She found herself chuckling under her breath. She had to give him credit for soliciting children to aide in his matchmaking work.

The organ continued to play and this time everyone joined in to sing 'Amazing Grace.' Becky found herself singing along. Usually she just listened, but today the words came over her and she couldn't help but feel the passion to sing. She didn't know how much time she had, and that fact made her understand how important her relationship with her Maker was. She always thought she had tomorrow to do better about praying and praising God, but the truth was— there might not be a tomorrow. Becky swallowed hard and tried to hold back her emotions. Father Joe motioned with his hands for the congregation to all sit.

Kenny stretched and put his right arm on the pew behind her. His crisp white shirt and dark blue suit coat didn't mask the muscles underneath. She felt them through all of his clothes against her thin dress. She jumped a tad and glanced over at Kenny. When he looked at her, she felt the heat rise to her cheeks.

Father said a few words out of the Bible and then ordered, "Rise, and sing the next song. Number one-o-one in your song books."

They all stood to sing. Becky straightened her lavender dress. She usually wore darker colors, but this morning she felt like something brighter, more alive. She no longer liked the color black. It was a color of mourning and that was the last thing she wanted to be reminded of right now.

"You look beautiful in that color," Kenny whispered next to her ear.

She stopped singing for a second, not knowing what to say and finally leaned over to whisper in Kenny's ear. "Thank you."

She could smell the scent of his soap. Becky always loved his soap. It smelled so much like a man and always made her want to… she shook her head to clear her thoughts. She shouldn't be thinking such things in church. What would God say? What would Father Joe say or Sister Margaret Mary?

Kenny leaned down a little as if sensing her feelings and she felt his fingers intertwine with her own. He was holding her hand. Just that slightest touch made her light-headed. Becky thought she would be over him by now, but instead of the three years closing the door on that emotion, it seemed to only intensify her feelings. She likened it to when she gave up chocolate for Lent one year for the Easter season and when Lent was over… chocolate never tasted better or sweeter. She felt the emotion tighten her throat.

Becky wanted to pull her fingers out of his grasp. This was the first time they'd touched like this since before their divorce. It didn't seem right now. They weren't married anymore. This was something people who were 'together' did. Reluctantly, she untangled her fingers and pretended to rifle through her purse looking for some money to put into the collection plate. The money was sitting in the side pocket ready, but she needed an excuse to compose herself and get her hand away from his touch. With the stroke of his fingers, her brain would always go foggy and her reasoning would fly out the window. That was why it took so long for her to leave the marriage. Every time she was about to leave, he would touch her or kiss her and she would melt and forget about all the problems and frustrating things that drove her crazy about him.

"I had another sermon prepared for today about the importance of tithing, however, I've decided to change the sermon to cover the commitment of marriage and what the Bible says about marriage..." Father Joe began his speech.

Becky groaned. Father Joe's speech was going to make the feelings she was having toward Kenny stronger. She knew the good Father did it on purpose, and she had to give him credit again for his perseverance. He'd taken it pretty personal when she'd told him about the divorce. She supposed in a way he thought of her like family since he'd known her for her entire life.

The choir singing the closing song interrupted her thoughts. The mass was ended. She loved church, but being like this seemed like sweet torture, a torture she couldn't allow herself to indulge in. It wasn't her right to indulge in it again.

Becky stood and put a hand on each one of the boy's shoulders. "Have I told you today how much I love you both?" Becky leaned down and kissed each one on the head.

"I love you, too. You tell us all the time, Mom." Justin grinned, dimples winking, and rolled his eyes.

"Yeah, but I like hearing it," Adam said as he gave his mother a hug.

"Thank you for asking me to church today," Becky said as they headed out of the pew.

"Do you have to leave, Mom?" Adam asked with a sad look.

"I'll see you both soon." Becky tried to make light of the dark cloud that suddenly loomed over them. The boys never did well with this type of thing. They despised the separate times and going separate ways.

"I hate that you and Dad aren't together!" Adam stomped his foot in a fit of temper and ran to the back of the church. Adam was always the one with the temper.

"Why can't it be like the old days when you and Dad were together? It's just not fair," Justin echoed his resentment of his parent's divorce, and instead of stomping his foot like his brother, he burst into tears. She watched with heartbreak as Justin ran to the back of church as well.

Becky gazed up at Kenny with wide sad eyes, not knowing what to say. Kenny just looked down at her with the same sadness. "It's been hard on them lately. Kids at school are starting to give them trouble about us being divorced. You know divorce isn't as acceptable and common in Catholic school. We're the only parents in the class that aren't married."

"What do you suppose we do about that?" she asked, slightly irritated. Life happened. Family units weren't all the same nowadays.

"The boys need both of us around. They need us together... married."

"But that's not an option."

"Isn't it?" Kenny raised a reddish eyebrow. "Why isn't it an option? You heard Father talk about marriage. We should've tried harder to make it work. We can try again, you know. It's just a piece of paper. One that can be reversed and ripped up. It's not written in stone that there aren't second chances."

"Kenny, why now after three years are you talking like this?"

"Because you're the one who seemed to open a window a crack for me to get back in. I've been knocking and trying all of this time. We've asked you to go out to eat with us many times over the years and you've always said no. The boys asked you to go to church with us and I can't count how many times you said no. I've been trying all along, you've had the door bolted and double-locked until recently. I've finally seen a way back into your life and heart. All I'm asking you is to give me a chance. Open the window more... or better yet, unlock the door."

She thought about what he said and knew he was right. She might've been trying to fool herself into thinking that

Kenny had been trying harder lately out of the blue, but what he said was true. She'd turned them down dozens of times over the years. Now, she found herself saying 'yes' to their invitations and to spending time with them. Saying yes to that precious time.

"We should go find the boys and see if they're all right." Becky motioned toward the back of church.

"The boys are fine. I saw Father Joe with them."

"Great, he'll be filling their heads even more with thoughts of what marriage should be like, just like the sermon he did for our benefit today," Becky said with some bitterness. "Maybe they're concocting a new plan to get us together like that old switcheroo in the pew the boys pulled."

"Becky, Father Joe just cares about us."

She groaned with frustration. "What could a man who's never been married know about being married?"

Kenny burst out laughing. "Probably more than I did. I did a horrible job. I wish I knew then what I know now. I would've helped you clean toilets, do the laundry, scrub floors, and made you candlelight dinners a little more often."

"A little more often?" Becky raised her eyebrow.

"Okay. I would've done those types of things for you at least once," Kenny said sheepishly.

Becky shrugged, a light lifting of her shoulders. "I'm not without fault myself. I should've compromised with you about the time you spent playing sports with your buddies. I was just jealous and tired, and to be honest, young."

"Yes, now you're so old," Kenny teased, a hand on her shoulder and then the teasing vanished as his voice became serious. "And to be honest, as you say, I wasn't there for you and the boys. I missed out on so much by hanging with my friends having beers during the game and after the game. I lived like a bachelor rather than a husband and father."

"There had to be a solution or compromise for both of us to be happy. I didn't try to find it. Instead, I grew more and more resentful of you being gone and not helping while you grew more and more resentful of me nagging about you being gone and not helping. Maybe we could've played on a co-ed team and got a babysitter or you could've played one night a week instead of three and four nights and I could've gone out one night with the girls so I could've gotten out, too. I don't know." Becky ran a tired hand through her long black hair. "It no longer matters now anyway."

"It's strange, but now I have an entire week at a time without the kids and you and I find myself not wanting to do those things I thought I wanted and needed to do before. I find myself wanting to be at home with you and the boys," Kenny admitted with sadness in his voice. "I guess it is true what they say about hindsight being twenty-twenty. And I guess it's true that I was a big fat butthead."

"I think we should go get our children. What we say doesn't change the past, doesn't change a thing, really. It might help us understand how we got here to this place, but it won't bring us back to where we were, where we should be," Becky said as she walked toward the rear of church.

Becky saw Justin and Adam talking to Father. She walked over and knelt down on the ground in front of them. "I'm sorry things aren't the way you would like them to be or the way they should be. All I can promise you is that Daddy and I love you and will always love you."

Justin nodded and then Adam nodded. Kenny walked up behind her and put his hand on her shoulder. "Your mother and I are friends and we'll try harder to do things more often as a group together, if you understand it's not because we're getting back together, but because we want to try to spend more time with you both. Does that sound fair?"

Adam nodded, a lump in his throat. "Yes." His voice still had a touch of an edge to it, but he allowed himself to be pulled into a hug.

Justin wiped his nose on the back of his hand and then threw his arms around his parents and his brother. Soon it was a family hug, even though they were no longer really technically a family, but it felt like it for one moment in time.

Becky glanced up and saw Father Joe watching them, a smile on his lips that was a mix of satisfaction and a touch of sadness. She knew he wanted them back together and to him this was probably a start, but it was no win.

Six

Monday came regardless of how hard she tried to wish it away. Every time the phone rang, she didn't know if she wanted to answer it or not. A part of her wanted to get this over with and find out what she already knew in her heart and the other part wanted to live in denial and hope a little bit longer. It seemed like all of her friends were calling wondering about the MRI test. Andrea, Carmen, Tammy Jane and, of course, her parents. Her parents had retired to Florida a while back and now lived in Watercolor. Becky had never seen a more beautiful place with such nice people. She loved it so much she had to get married there and her parents loved it so much they decided to move there when they officially retired. It was a place you never wanted to leave.

The phone rang yet again, interrupting her thoughts. Becky jumped, pausing a second and said a prayer—and then answered the phone with a tentative, "Hello?"

"Becky Winroy?" a professional sounding voice asked briskly before introducing himself. "This is Dr. Verdin."

"Yes?"

"I'm sorry to have to tell you this, but we have the results of your MRI we performed a couple of days ago…"

Becky lost her breath and felt the room begin to spin. The cordless phone was pressed against her ear with her right hand while her left hand gripped the sofa so she wouldn't fall over. She heard a voice that sounded exactly like hers say, "Yes?"

She was an educated woman, however, all that she could manage was the word 'yes.'

"We found a brain tumor," Dr. Verdin said in rehearsed voice. She was sure he sadly said this many times over in his career.

She wondered if there was a training class that doctors went to, to learn how to tell someone things like this, she wondered. Did they practice in front of a mirror or rehearse speeches in front of other doctors to inform their patients they were dying or a loved one had died?

"Malignant or benign?" Becky asked calmly. She couldn't believe how steady her voice sounded. She finally found something in her brain to actually say a word other than 'yes.' However, she liked the word 'yes' better than the word malignant. The word 'yes' seemed more cheery and hopeful.

"Malignant or better known as cancerous. You have a primary brain tumor on the base of your skull. A primary brain tumor is a tumor that begins in the brain. Some other brain tumors start somewhere else like the lungs or the breasts and spread to the brain, those are called secondary brain tumors…"

She knew Dr. Verdin was saying lots of other important things but only bits and pieces of sentences and words drifted through the fog that had suddenly taken over her mind. Becky heard 'operate as soon as possible' and many other frightening action words mixed with large medical vocabulary words.

Again, she heard a familiar voice say, barely recognizing it as her own, "Thank you for calling, Dr. Verdin."

Her finger hit the button to hang up and then the phone fell to the floor with a muffled clunk. Becky held on to the sofa and lowered herself to floor. Her stomach began to roll and the contents of her stomach spewed all over the plush white carpet. The foul stain messing up her beautiful white carpet no longer mattered to her. She always liked her house spotless like her mother taught her, but spotless just didn't seem important right now. Her mother's teaching didn't prepare her for a moment like this. There was no class on how to handle such devastating news. No instruction as she was growing up on how to react to such a thing. Sure, there were directions on how to ride a bike, lectures on not doing drugs or driving under the influence of alcohol…. But nothing for a life-threatening moment like this.

Becky didn't know how long she stayed on the floor surrounded by the offensive mess. The phone rang many times somewhere in the distance. It didn't matter. The room turned dark—that didn't matter either. Did day or night really matter? Did doing the dishes really matter? Did cleaning up the carpet really matter?

She had no idea what time it was when she heard the door click. She just watched it open. Before she would've been scared about a burglar, however, now a robbery was the least of her worries. Let him take everything she owned, she thought. Her collection of priceless original art and blown glass now seemed like a waste of time and money. She couldn't take it with her. The criminal breaking in would benefit more from it than she would. He probably had a drug habit to pay for.

"Becky?" a voice called from the darkness.

In her condition, she didn't feel like answering. So what the intruder knew her name? Maybe he did his homework before breaking into people's homes. An educated burglar. She couldn't work up the strength to even laugh.

"Becky? It's me, Kenny."

She didn't answer, couldn't answer.

"Andrea called me and was worried about you. She's been trying to call you for hours. Carmen called in a panic as well. They were going to come over, but I said I'd check on you." There was silence and then a light flipping on, followed by an astonished gasp, "Becky! Are you all right? Should I call for an ambulance?"

Becky managed to shake her head slightly. She wanted to answer Kenny and tell him she was fine. She wanted to, but nothing came out of her mouth.

"What happened? Do you have the flu?" Kenny asked, brushing a strand of hair away from her face.

Again, she moved her head with the slightest of movements.

"Food poisoning?" Kenny asked as he took the snowy white blanket off the back of the couch and wrapped it around her shoulders, easing her to her feet.

"No," she said in a whispered breath.

"Let me get you to bed." He guided her toward the master bedroom.

It wasn't long before she was tucked between the cool sheets. She didn't even care that Kenny had undressed her and slipped her nightshirt on. She heard him say something about her clothes being soiled.

"Becky? Please say something," Kenny pleaded as he held her limp hand. She wanted to. She wanted to blurt out all her problems. She wanted to lean her head against his shoulder and soak up the comfort she knew was there. But wanting and doing were two separate things.

She watched through the window of her mind as he placed her hand on the bed and headed for the bathroom. She watched him come back, a washcloth in his hand. Becky felt the cool cloth on her forehead. It seemed to bring her out of the cloud a little. Enough to finally manage to ask in a weak voice, "The boys?"

"The boys are with Andrea. I dropped them off on the

way over here. I wasn't sure what… I wasn't sure what I'd find," Kenny said honestly. "It's unlike you not to answer the phone. I didn't know if there was a break-in or if you were hurt. Are you hurt?"

She could see worry in Kenny's eyes. She was filled with hurt. Her heart hurt with the fear of not seeing her children grow up. Her head hurt from the overwhelming processing on what the doctor said on the phone.

"Not really," she finally answered. "I'm just a mess." Becky turned her head away so he couldn't see her face.

He took her jaw gently in his palm and turned it back. "When I see you, I never see anything but beauty."

"Kenny…" Becky's eyes started to water. She didn't want to put him through what was about to happen to her. The surgery. The chemo. It wasn't his responsibility or burden to carry. It was hers to carry alone. She'd made her bed years ago when she divorced him and that bed is where she must lie. Alone.

"Kenny, please leave. I'm fine now," she insisted unconvincingly.

"You are not fine. What happened tonight?"

"I don't want to talk about it," Becky said with clenched teeth, her head beginning to pound.

"Becky…"

"My doctor called." Becky turned her head back away, unable to meet his questioning eyes.

"What did he say?"

Becky could tell by his tone he already suspected. A big part of her had already known before she received the phone call. It was just hearing the words out loud that sent her into shock. Hearing the doctor confirm made her condition seem so much more real.

"He said that I have a primary brain tumor and need immediate surgery. I'm supposed to go in tomorrow at ten o'clock," she sighed and then added, "He said a bunch of other things that I didn't understand or hear."

"He scheduled surgery already for tomorrow?" Kenny was stunned.

"Yep. I'm not supposed to eat. I guess I've got that covered since I threw up the contents of my stomach all over the floor." She tried to sound flippant but he saw right through her.

"He scheduled the surgery for tomorrow at ten?" he repeated.

"Yes. The surgery is at ten. Are you having trouble hearing?" Becky mocked loudly as if talking to an elderly person who was nearly deaf.

"Are your parents coming in?"

"I haven't called them yet. They don't know anything of what's going on," Becky admitted. "I don't want to upset them any more than necessary." She knew she should've called them, but why? She could get through this. It was just surgery, after all. "I can handle this and I'll be fine on my own. It's better that no one knows about the surgery. It's better that I'm alone."

"But you're not alone. You have lots of friends who love you and you have me." Kenny rubbed her hand softly.

"The thing is... I just want to be alone right now. Please just go," Becky said in a flat unemotional voice.

"I don't care what you want. I'm not leaving you alone tonight and I'm not leaving you ever," Kenny said firmly as he slipped under the covers and took her limp body into his arms. She drew comfort from the warmth against her cool lifeless body.

She tried to push him away, but he held her even more tightly. She gave up and sobbed in his arms. Sometime after three in the morning, she finally fell asleep in the circle of his strong embrace.

"Your wife has an anaplastic meningioma," Dr. Verdin explained to Kenny as Becky lay on the patient table. Meningiomas represent about twenty percent of all primary brain tumors and occur more often in women." She felt like she was on an island and about ready to fall off. Instead of being soft sand, it was hard plastic.

"Why didn't she have more signs before now?" Kenny asked.

"Well, the type of tumor she has is slow growing and the majority of people who have them never know about them until something raises suspicion, like in your wife's case, headaches and some vision problems," Dr. Verdin told him in a professional tone.

"I just thought the headaches and vision problems were from stress or from bending over my computer working all the time," she confessed. "It never dawned on me that I had a brain tumor. I just chalked it up to being young and over-worked."

"You can have double vision, weakness, numbness, a headache that is worse upon waking and clears up within a few hours and even vomiting and confusion."

"Who are you?" Becky looked at Kenny and tried to joke, but the joke fell flat.

"Not funny," Kenny told her, tapping her nose.

"Dr. Verdin seems to think you're my husband. I thought I got confused and forgot that we've been divorced for three years," Becky commented, again trying to be funny, but failing.

"You're not being funny. I know you're nervous and you always try to lighten the mood with your awful jokes and humor," Kenny said as he stroked her hair. "Don't. It isn't necessary."

"My, aren't you forceful?" Becky gave Kenny a crooked strained smile. She did have a way of dealing with stress with fake humor.

"I apologize, I thought you had re-married." Dr. Verdin looked down at the chart and pointed to a document she'd filled out recently on her medical history and patient information. Sure enough, she'd checked the box that said 'Mrs.'

and she had written Kenny's name in for husband. She felt a flush of heat creep across her cheeks.

Kenny looked down at her, brows arched. "I'd say that was a Freudian slip, but I'm guessing you already know that."

Her face turned a bright crimson with embarrassment. He was probably right. On some subconscious level, she must've wanted him to be her husband. She didn't have time to psychoanalyze the matter right now.

"Sorry, Dr. Verdin," Becky apologized. "I just checked the wrong box. Kenny is still my ex-husband."

"Well, in my opinion, you both look like you belong together. Perhaps you want a moment to talk before you get prepped for surgery?" Dr. Verdin asked, not caring if he was overstepping his bounds.

"I'm still wondering how you got me into surgery so quickly. Can't all of this wait a week or two?" Becky stalled.

"The quicker we tackle this, the better chance we have. So, no time like today," Dr. Verdin said as he stood up. "Dr. Shelden is performing the surgery and I'm just scrubbing up to be present."

She nodded in affirmation. It was nice to have someone close by who actually knew her for more than a chart and a name. The good doctor left the room.

Becky looked up at Kenny and fidgeted. "I'm sorry for everything over the years. I wish I would've been a better wife to you."

"Becky, you were a great wife to me. I was never home and when I was, I forgot how to be romantic, but why don't we stop talking about the past? Why don't we just focus on the here and now?"

"Where are the boys?" Becky asked with tears in her eyes. "Are they still at Andrea's?"

"No, Andrea brought them to the hospital. I called her and told her what was going on this morning. They're in the waiting room with the entire cheering section. Of course, led by non other than the cheerleader herself ... Andrea."

"Andrea is here at the hospital? I didn't think she would come. She hates hospitals. She even delivered her children at home to avoid a hospital," Becky said, feeling worried about her friend, knowing it must be hard on her to be here.

"She's keeping occupied watching Chloe and our children. Besides, I don't think she would be any other place. You've been best friends forever," Kenny pointed out.

She became aware of how he had cute little fan lines around his eyes. His face was so young looking, but the fan lines now gave a clue to his getting older. She always marveled how he was always carded when they went into any bar or to buy alcohol when they were married.

"I should go and let the nurses take care of you." Kenny voiced the words, but his grip was still on her hand.

Becky sighed heavily. "Can you keep talking to me? Your voice soothes me."

"I'd think you would hate my voice, just like you grew to hate me over the years."

"Hate you?" Becky asked in surprise. "You actually think I grew to hate you?"

"Well, you avoid me every chance you get. We've been dropping the kids off at neutral locations for the past three years. I'm guessing so you won't have to see where I live and you don't want me anywhere near the house. I think it's pretty obvious how much you hate me."

The nurse came in and after inserting an IV into her arm, held up a razor and a pair of scissors. "I hate to tell you this, but the doctor wants me to shave a part of your head so he can perform the surgery. I need to shave the back of the scalp."

She didn't know what to say. How do you respond to that? Her hair had been long for as long as she could remember. It was what Kenny said he loved about her and what made him notice her when they were at the fair when they were just kids.

The nurse asked, "Can you sit up, please?"

Becky nodded and pushed to a sitting position. She noticed the nurse had beautiful long hair as well. Ironic. The nurse cut Becky's long hair with scissors first so she could shave the area. She stared down at the hair falling around her like black rain and wanted to weep.

"Do you want me to try to save as much hair as possible?"

Save as much hair as possible? Becky nearly laughed. The hair that now lay on the floor had turned the white flooring into a soft black carpet. "No. Just shave me bald. It will look silly to have a part of it long and a part of it shaved. Just shear it all and be done with it," Becky said in a tight-lipped voice, trying to keep the hurt at bay. If she didn't have her head completely shaved, she'd look like she'd had a fight with a weed whacker and lost, she was thinking.

"Are you sure?" The nurse waited for an answer with the razor poised ready to finish the deed.

"I'm sure. It's just hair, right?" Becky said as she watched more clumps of her locks fall to the floor to join the others, the floor taking the shape of a black bear shag rug.

Kenny held her hand while the nurse became the barber. Nobody said a word, after all, what was there to say? Had the nurse had training in shearing heads? Was she thinking about her own long beautiful hair as she cut off Becky's?

The nurse quickly swept the hair into a dustpan and bustled out of the room as if hoping if she moved quickly enough, it would seem like the ordeal never happened.

Becky fidgeted with the IV tubing coming out of her arm. "I hate these stupid plastic things. It reminds me of straws." She glanced up at Kenny, frowning, the distress showing plainly on her features.

"Becky, I'm sorry you lost your hair. I'm guessing you feel very afraid right now ... afraid of the surgery."

She ran a hand over her now smooth scalp. Kids in her high school used to shave their heads for a statement. She had hers shaved because of brain surgery. High school was so long ago. Things seemed hard then, but in reality were so much simpler. Becky reached up and lightly touched Kenny's face with her fingertips. "Actually, it's probably the opposite. I'm not at all afraid of the surgery. What will be, will be. What I am afraid of is if I'm alone for too long with you, I'll start realizing what a stupid mistake I made giving you up. When we're alone, I forget all about reasoning and what I feel for you takes over and..."

"Time for your surgery, Miss Winroy," said a cute redheaded nurse with flowing hair as she motioned for Kenny to leave. "And time, handsome, for you to go. Your ex-wife is in good hands." What was it with everyone having long hair? Becky thought resentfully.

Becky tasted something that she wasn't used to tasting. Jealousy. The nurse was flirting with Kenny—her Kenny. She couldn't believe what she was thinking. Kenny wasn't hers anymore and there was no reason she should be jealous. Yet, here it was. That green-eyed monster clawing at her insides. She'd been the one who'd cast him back into the sea of single men. Becky tilted her head to the side and frowned. The nurse looked vaguely familiar then she gasped in disbelief. The nurse was the woman in the leopard bikini from the swimming party at Carmen's house! She was a nurse? She should've figured that with her luck lately...

"I'll go." He nodded at the nurse and smiled at Becky, then bent forward and brushed her cheek with a soft kiss. She realized how handsome he still was. The leopard suit nurse was practically fainting over him. But oddly, Kenny didn't seem to notice. He just kept looking at Becky.

"Go on," she urged. "I'll be fine. I just wish I could give Adam and Justin a kiss ... just in case..."

Kenny surprised her by having tears in his eyes. "There won't be a 'just in case.' You'll be just fine. I can bring the boys in if you want to give them a kiss just because you love them."

"I would love that, but I don't want to scare them looking like this. Just tell them I love them, that I love them more than anything in the world ... and Kenny..."

"Yes?" Kenny wiped a fallen drop from his cheek.

"If I come through this," Becky sniffed, "I'm going to change."

"You're perfect the way you are."

"If I was so perfect why didn't you want to be at home more often with me and the kids? Why didn't you send me roses and watch the sunset with me? I wasn't perfect. I'd like to try to be, if God gives me a second chance." She used the back of her hand as a Kleenex and then yelped as the taped tubing pulled her skin with the movement.

"Did I tell you how much I hate needles and hospitals?" Becky asked in a tear-filled voice.

"I know." Kenny kissed her forehead. "You know, this is the second hardest thing I've ever had to do, watching them wheel you away like this."

"What's the very hardest thing you had to do?" Curiosity got the best of her and she had to ask.

"The hardest thing was letting you go and giving you the freedom that you wanted. It killed me to sign those divorce papers."

"Kenny..."

"Time for you to go, Mr. Winroy," the leopard bikini nurse said a little briskly. It seemed like it was her turn to be jealous.

"Bye, Kenny."

"No, not bye. Never bye. How about we say hello instead? How does that sound?"

"Silly and a little odd, but all right." Becky nearly laughed. "Hello, Kenny."

"Hello, Becky."

The nurse wheeled her out of the room. She couldn't bear looking over her shoulder at Kenny, but gave in at the last moment and saw him kneeling on the floor with tears streaming down his face.

Becky offered up a silent prayer. "Dear God, please get me through this surgery and when I am healthy again, I promise to consider every day a blessing and every minute with the people I love special. Every sunrise and sunset a gift. Amen."

The bikini nurse pushed her into a waiting area and left her. Becky took the moment to glance around at her surroundings. She felt like she'd been herded into a holding pen for animals. It was one big area divided by curtains to make several smaller areas which reminded her of a horse stable—but less smelly and completely germ-free. She sighed. She'd gotten her wish. She was all alone and she was finding being alone wasn't all that great. Her gaze swept the area, stared at the sterile white walls. Someone should at least paint something fun on these walls, something to liven up the place so it wouldn't be so bleak. No one should have to go into surgery and possibly have the last moment on this earth looking at boring cheerless walls.

"Becky Winroy?"

"Yes?"

"I'm Dr. Shelden. I'm the doctor who's going to be performing your surgery…"

Seven

Her eyes slowly came into focus. She lay on her stomach. She moved her head slightly to look around the room and immediately pain ripped through her system. She knew she wasn't dead and in heaven. Heaven wouldn't have such excruciating pain like she was experiencing. Her gaze landed on Dr. Shelden's green booties over his shoes and she heard Dr. Verdin say, "Give her some more morphine to let her rest. Her vitals are good. It'll help with the headache she's going to have and help her endure the pain. She'll be in Intensive Care for a week once she leaves the recovery room."

Then she felt the blissful feeling of sleep overtake her and vanquished the pain. She was so tired, had never felt quite so weary. The smell of the recovery room slowly faded. Those green booties gradually turned to shadows.

The next time she woke she was in a different room. She must be in ICU now, she thought, as the fog slowly lifted from her mind. She saw lots of monitors and wires and she was still on her stomach. Becky didn't have the strength to really care what the room looked like or where the wires went to. This time she saw no feet. She just heard the beeping of machines and saw the whiteness of the floor.

Then everything started to fade like a dimming image that slowly disappeared on a television screen.

She opened her eyes again and white shoes crossed her vision, hands touching her in different places and checking her head, but it didn't really seem important. All that seemed important now was the delightful feeling she felt when the pain went away and she fell into a velvet darkness. Becky welcomed the darkness behind her eyelids.

This time she heard a woman's voice wearing tan shoes. "Everything seems to be healing" and "blood pressure is good" came the words in a whispering tone. Becky thought she heard a familiar deep voice talking to her as well, but she couldn't stay awake long enough to answer. The masculine tone echoed through her dreams and filled her heart. It was soothing like the voice the day she had the MRI. A voice that gave her peace in a time when she so desperately needed peace. A voice that she loved.

She opened her eyes to bright light. Her perspective had changed from shoes to ceiling tiles. It looked more like a regular old hospital room. She decided to just move her eyeballs and not her head just in case. She let her gaze roam the room as best she could and she let out a soft gasp. The entire room was filled with the most beautiful roses she had ever seen. She blinked again to clear her vision to make sure it wasn't just a dream.

It wasn't a dream. They were still there. The roses displayed dazzling color. They had sunny yellow highlights on the petals and at the base of the rose. Such a soft luscious pink offsetting the yellow. It was a pink almost like an apricot or peach color. The roses looked exactly like a sunset. Tears spilled into her eyes as she stared around her. God had given her the gift to see another sunset, in this case, it was in the form of a rose with blushing shades of a sunset.

Kenny was sitting in the midst of all the roses sleeping in a purple chair. A small smile graced her lips. He was here. She tried to reach for him, but her arm was heavy and she was weak. Becky tried to talk, but her throat was too dry. She finally managed, "Kenny…" in a hoarse cracked syllable.

He must've sensed her, for he certainly couldn't have heard her faint cry. Kenny opened his eyes and sat up quickly, immediately rushing to her side. "Bec?"

She tried to clear her throat again and this time her voice was a tad better. "The roses? You?"

"I wanted to give you a sunset."

"What?" She didn't understand. She didn't know if it was the pain medicine or the fact that she was recovering from the effects of the surgery.

"The roses. The florist called them Tahitian Sunset Roses. I believe they're a hybrid tea rose, according to the florist anyway." Kenny gave her a big smile. "They were delivered this morning and I bought every one she had. It was fate. What are the chances the florist would get a shipment of a flower that said everything I wanted to say to you when you woke up?"

"Too expensive," she scolded. She knew he had a budget. He made all right money, but not enough to splurge like this.

"Becky, let me have this moment. A moment that says I'm sorry. A moment that says that I'm so happy that you've made it through surgery and a moment that allows me to give you a sunset and a rose at the same time."

She said softly, "Sorry." She didn't want to spoil the moment and added with effort, "Liquorish?"

Kenny looked confused for a second, then grinned. "Yes. The roses smell like liquorish. I wanted you to wake up to something other than the antiseptic smell of a hospital. You know you've been sleeping for a long time. I…"

Becky interrupted, "The boys?"

"Andrea took them home with her while you were recovering in ICU. The doctor didn't want you to have a lot of visitors. I hope that was okay."

"It's fine," she said breathlessly as she looked again at the roses and marveled how long of a stem they had. The stems were over a foot long and the flowers themselves were of a considerable size as well. It was an amazing sight. She could barely see the entire rose from her prone position. "You stayed?" She wasn't sure hearing him when she was fading in and out of sleep was in her dreams yet or not.

Kenny nodded and said softly, "I never left your side."

"Most beautiful roses … ever seen," Becky rasped in a voice weak.

"In all their beauty, they don't compare to you," Kenny told her, taking her hand gently in his, being careful of the tubes.

"Cheesy, but nice…" She smiled and closed her eyes and drifted back into a medicated sleep.

Becky struggled into Kenny's truck with support from her ex-husband. The hospital aide assisted with placing all the roses into the vehicle and nodded his goodbyes as he pushed the wheelchair back toward the hospital.

As she sat in the truck, she found it almost ironic that not long ago she didn't want to ride with him—that she actually drove separately to the pizza restaurant to avoid the intimacy of a small confined area. Yet, here she was on the seat next to him with all of her roses surrounding her looking like a beauty queen's backdrop. Becky gingerly touched the bandage on her head. She was no beauty queen. The leopard bikini woman might be considered one, but she was most definitely not. There would never be a bald beauty queen.

"You look striking surrounded by all those roses,"

Kenny told her as he climbed into the driver's seat.

Becky peeked around a rose. "I would say that you're full of..."

"Easy there, sailor, I think you've gotten a little spunkier since your stay in the hospital." Kenny grinned broadly and gave her a wink. "Not that this man doesn't mind spunky."

"If you keep up all this sweet talk and rose giving, you're going to end up wooing me back." Becky tried to make light of her words, but despite her light tone, she was dead serious.

"I'll make a note of that," Kenny said with a smile as they drove away from the hospital. "It seems that I can use all the help I can get on that front."

Becky wanted to make some comment about them being divorced, but she just didn't have the energy to tackle that bear. She'd used up all her energy tackling the surgery and recovery in the hospital. It hadn't been easy. All she could say now was that one part of her path was done and the next one was just getting ready to begin. She had to go through treatment to make sure the surgery remained a success. Dr. Shelden told her after the surgery that everything went as perfectly as possible, that the tumors were removed completely. However, of course, chemotherapy was a must. Becky didn't like being told what was a 'must.' She hated being told what to do. It made her want to rebel and do the opposite. She knew that was crazy, but it was human nature—her human nature.

She glanced into the side mirror. She already had the hair loss part done. Many women had to wait and worry about that happening, she had it over and done with—maybe it was a blessing ... maybe it wasn't. Becky touched her smooth head in the front, the back of her head still bandaged from surgery. She looked very much like a soldier of war. She supposed in an odd way she was. The war in this case was an invisible opponent—cancer.

"Your head is beautiful with or without hair," Kenny said as he looked at her for a long moment, then focused his attention back on the road.

"If you like that turtle-shell look."

"I like any look on you." He reached under the seat and pulled out a small bag. "I was saving it for later, but now seems like a good time."

She took the white bag and opened it up. She didn't know what to say. Inside was the prettiest scarf she'd ever seen. It looked like a rainbow had kissed the soft cotton and left its mark.

"I hope you like it. The bright colors reminded me of your personality," Kenny stated in a tone thick with emotion. "And the saleslady said it would match everything."

"I love it." She took the multi-hued material and wrapped it around her bald head. This time when she looked into the truck mirror, someone different stared back. Someone wiser and more mature—almost beautiful in an eclectic sort of way ... almost.

"Why is life so backward?" Becky asked out of nowhere.

"Backward?"

"Well, you race and race to get through it when you're young and miss out on so much because you don't have the wisdom to enjoy it. Then when you're older, you're wiser and able to appreciate life, but your body is too tired to do all the things that are fun. You really can appreciate life or people to the fullest when you are young," Becky said as she fiddled with her wedding ring.

"Are you saying you're too old to have fun anymore?" Kenny asked with a curve of his lips. "Old is a state of mind, not of body."

"I feel old in my mind *and* my body."

"What do you expect, you just had brain surgery. It's bound to make anyone feel old," Kenny stated the obvious.

"I mean, I feel like my life is closing and no matter how hard I try, I'm slipping down that path that everyone tries to avoid heading down."

"I think all you need is some high-quality rest and great cooking and you'll feel young and good as new, maybe even younger than the thirty-four years that you are."

"I hate to tell you this, but Justin and Adam can only microwave macaroni and cheese and sadly, I'm not in the best shape yet to whip myself up some of those great meals," Becky said, resting her head against the back of the seat. Her body trembled from exhaustion. If she remembered correctly, this was her week to watch the children. How was she to do that when she felt this rotten?

She felt terrible and so frail. She wasn't even sure how she was going to take care of the boys since it was her turn. She cringed at that pronoun. It shouldn't be like this. The idea of a divorce had sounded like such a great and all-wise decision when she came up with it, but now after three years, she wasn't so sure how great that decision had been. It seemed like leaving Kenny would solve all the problems. All it did was add new problems along with the old problems.

"Are you forgetting someone else who can cook for you?" Kenny asked in a slightly offended tone.

"You? You are going to cook for me?" Becky said in disbelief. He'd never cooked while they were married. She'd done everything herself. She didn't even think he knew how to boil water for macaroni.

"Yes, me. I'm going to cook for you."

"I'll be fine. Andrea or Carmen can come in and cook for me. They even offered to stay with me. If they can't do it, Tammy Jane said she would fly in from California and spend a week helping. She has vacation time she can use and no children to worry about juggling."

Becky hated to ask Tammy Jane to use her time off to take care of her sick friend, but she might be forced to do so. Tammy Jane had said she needed a break anyway from all the craziness of Hollywood law and welcomed spending time catching up with friends. Becky believed that could be partially true, but no one probably wanted to use their coveted relaxation time to slave over a sick person. Friend or not.

"Bec, let's be honest. Andrea is so tiny that she'll never be able to pick you up if you need help or be able to assist you with anything…like to the bathroom or shower," Kenny reasoned. "And Carmen isn't much taller. She barely measures in at five-foot five."

She bit at her nails. It was one of those bad habits she found herself doing when she was nervous or upset. "Shower? Toilet? I think I'll be just fine taking care of those things on my own."

"You just had surgery. You've spent a week in ICU and two weeks in all at the hospital. You can barely sit up. You're going to need just a tad bit of help for a while."

"Tammy Jane is taller than me. She's almost six-foot. I'll just have to ask her," Becky put in reluctantly.

"Yes, she probably could take care of you, but do you really want her going to all that trouble to fly down here under those terms? It would probably be better to have her come down for a visit when you feel better and could actually catch up on old times and have fun… that is if you're not too old for fun."

She sighed. Kenny was saying things she already knew and thought of. Sadly, she had to admit he was right. She still floundered like a fish. "What…what…what about my parents?"

"Bec, your dad just had his hip replaced. He couldn't even come on the plane because of the pain he'd be in. Even if your mother flew in without him, there's no one to take care of him down there with her gone," Kenny pointed out.

"I know. She was crushed when I made them promise not to come visit me in the hospital. She cried on the phone forever begging me to say yes, to let her come. I almost caved and said she could, but I knew since my dad just had the surgery to fix his hip, it was best for them to stay put,"

Becky said somberly.

It killed her not to have her parents by her side, but what could they really do anyway? She told her mom just to pray and that would be more than enough. Her prayers must've worked because she was sitting, well, half-scrunched on this truck seat today.

"The most logical person is me," Kenny stated firmly.

"Kenny, we're not married."

"You don't need to keep reminding me of that fact. I'm not proposing this as a way to win you back. I am just trying to help you, the mother of my children. We were best friends once, remember?" Kenny looked over at her quickly and then back to the road.

"I remember."

"What if you fall and hit your head? What if you have problems related to the surgery? Do you want to risk that because of your stubbornness? I think you're being selfish. Is that fair to our boys who need a mother?"

"No," Becky murmured.

"It's settled then. I'm staying at the house."

The rest of the ride back to her house, *their old house*, was done in silence. Kenny pulled up front and then went around to her side to open the door. He slipped his strong arms around her and lifted her easily. She started to protest, but even that small movement made the scenery around her look like a giant whirl pool. It kept swirling and swirling.

"Are you all right?" Kenny asked with concern in his voice.

"I think the motion of the truck, mixed with the movement from you is making me feel sick."

Kenny took the key out of his pocket to unlock the door. She'd given it to him in case of any emergencies or if he needed to get anything of the boys for some reason. She imagined lots of people probably thought that was odd to give your ex a key to your house, but at this time she was thankful she did.

"Kenny?"

"Yes?"

"I'm going to be sick," Becky said quietly.

She felt like a child on the tea cup ride at an amusement park, the tea cup whirling so fast the world looked like cotton candy spinning inside of the machine maker. She was the child who knew she would get sick at any moment but couldn't stop the cup from spinning. It was just a matter of time before the body controlled the mind.

Kenny whisked her inside and before she knew it she was sitting on the couch with a Tupperware bowl in her hands. The contents of her stomach, which consisted of hospital broth and crackers, emptied out.

"I'm so sorry." Becky looked up apologetically, momentarily granted a reprieve from the nausea but knew she was going to be sick again soon.

"Becky, I think I can handle you throwing up. I've taken care of the boys many times when they had the flu, and I've dealt with it at work. It's just a part of life. Nothing more."

That brief moment in time when the nausea took a hiatus passed and she became ill once more, vomiting into the bowl. When she finally felt that knot at the top of her stomach leave, she sat the container down and lay back on the couch for a minute until her head stop spinning. Becky always did hate the rides at amusement parks that spun and twirled. And the ride she felt she was on now, all she wanted was to get off. Tea cups were for kids, not adults.

Kenny picked up the Tupperware without any comments or facial expressions and walked into the bathroom to empty it and brought her a clean bowl. "Just in case you feel sick again."

"I think I feel better. I could've taken care of that." She nodded toward the now clean bowl.

"You could've, but why should you when I'm here?"

She managed to say, "Thank you."

Becky looked down at the carpet by the couch. It was spotless. There was no evidence of the night she threw up all over it. Kenny had cleaned it up well. It seemed like a lifetime ago that the doctor had called her to give the bad news. She supposed Kenny was right about that type of thing not bothering him. She saw him in a new light when she looked up and watched him walk away.

He soon came back with a pillow and sheet. He placed the pillow on the couch and lowered her down until the soft pillow touched her cheek. She had to be careful of her head and the healing incision. Then, with gentle hands, Kenny covered her up with the sheet.

Becky sighed. It had been a long three years. Maybe this was what marriage was all about—that feeling of comfort in the other person. She yawned and fell into a deep sleep.

When she woke, there was a delicious aroma circulating through the house. It smelled of chicken. She took a deep breath and was surprised when her stomach rumbled with hunger. Ever since her surgery, she hadn't felt like eating and any smell set her stomach churning. However, the smell of chicken today actually intrigued her senses.

Kenny must've heard her rustling and sing-songed, "Your chicken noodle soup is almost ready."

Chicken noodle soup? He must've just opened a can. Could a can of soup smell that good? She eased herself up into a semi-sitting position and groaned. She quickly lay back down, weak, with an aching head.

Kenny moved over and knelt next to her on the carpet with a hot steaming bowl of soup. He spooned up the liquid and blew on it like she'd done a hundred times for Justin and Adam when they were little. Then she watched as he moved the spoon towards her mouth.

"I can do it," she protested. This was way too intimate for people that were divorced.

"You're too weak," Kenny commented as he held the

spoon up to her mouth, waiting.

"I don't need you to take care of me."

"No, you don't. But I want to," he replied, his blue-green eyes bright and alert, watching her every move.

Becky opened her mouth and let the warm liquid trickle down her throat. The soup tasted quite good.

"Did you make this from scratch?" she asked doubtfully.

"I did."

"I wasn't asleep that long." She thought he was fibbing and actually either had the soup delivered from the local deli or found a canned soup that tasted wonderful. A lot of famous chefs now marketed their soups in cans. Could this be one of those soups?

"You've been asleep for eight hours," Kenny told her, pointing to the clock on the mantle.

"Oh!" she said in amazement as she looked at where he was pointing. Sure enough, it had been eight hours. The pain medicine they gave her before leaving the hospital had finally kicked in. However, a small part of her wondered if the reason she slept so well, was knowing Kenny was watching over her.

"I'm still thinking you didn't make this yourself. You couldn't even make toast while we were married. Prove it," Becky challenged.

"I did too make it," Kenny said, almost sounding like a child arguing. Then he smiled and said, "All right, I'll prove it."

"I'm waiting..." Becky couldn't help but tease.

"I cut up a small onion, three carrots and some celery. I threw them into a pot with oil and let it cook until they were soft. Then I poured in chicken broth and added the chicken. I let that boil and finally dropped in four fresh springs of parsley, three fresh springs of thyme and a bay leaf."

"Where did you get the fresh herbs?" Becky tested.

"From your herbs that you have in pots on the back screened-in porch," Kenny answered easily.

"How did you know which spice was which?" she asked, arching an eyebrow.

"You have them marked on the front of each pot. I can read, you know." Kenny laughed.

"Fine, go on." Becky waited for the rest of the recipe.

"I just turned down the heat to let it simmer for two hours until everything was tender. I added salt and pepper and then the noodles and voila. Homemade chicken noodle soup," Kenny said with a bow.

She nodded her head, impressed. "Very good. The recipe … where did you get that from?"

"I took some cooking classes over the years at the community college. I'm actually quite a good cook if you must know."

Cooking classes? She didn't know he'd taken those. When had that happened? she frowned. Maybe he was trying to impress some woman he was dating or interested in. She noticed he'd even garnished the top of the soup with sprinkles of parsley. She didn't think he was lying about the cooking class. He fed her another bite.

"I'm sure that all your girlfriends love the meals," Becky said, trying not to show any emotion in her voice. However, she was sure that a tinge of jealousy crept in.

"Girlfriends?" Kenny repeated and laughed, "Heavens, no. There's only been one girlfriend that I've had."

"Oh." She was sorry she asked. One girlfriend was worse than many girlfriends because with one, he must be serious and with many, it meant he hadn't found that certain special 'one.'

"I've learned a lot over these past three years. I had to learn to cook to feed the boys something besides frozen dinners and pizza delivery. It's something I should've learned a long time ago and helped you out more while we were married." Kenny gave a sad half-smile as he blew on another spoonful. "You were always a great cook and took care of everything. I guess I just depended on you and took advantage of you doing it all. I'm ashamed to say that I watched as you cooked every meal, did all the cleaning, washing, pay bills and I even let you mow the grass and do the yard work all the while you took care of the twins and grew your company. All I did was work at my job and play sports and watch sports. You basically had three children to take care of instead of the two you should've had."

"I managed just fine."

"You managed, but maybe if I would've helped out more, we wouldn't be in this place in our lives. Divorced," Kenny said sadly.

"Maybe, but what's done is done. We're both happier now. I'm happier now," Becky emphasized. Her voice sounded doubtful to her own ears.

"Are we really happier?" Kenny asked, one eyebrow raised as if also hearing the doubt in her voice.

"You help me out now because the judge told you to. You have certain days you're responsible for. In a way, it's been easier and allowed me more time to myself and to be more successful in my work." Becky was telling the truth about that, but she wasn't sure that truth made her happier. She did have more help now because of joint custody of their children, however, she strangely missed her old life right about now.

"I'm still amazed how you raised the twins, took care of everything and made your companies very successful. You must've been exhausted."

She shrugged and repeated, "I managed. But isn't that what men expect out of women… to do it all?"

If Carmen would've heard that sentence she would be high-fiving her friend at the moment for making such a liberal statement. Carmen thought that women should rule the world. If Andrea had heard, she would be shaking her head at such thinking. She was more old-fashioned and believed that a woman's place was in the home taking care of her house, husband and children. Becky didn't fault Andrea for her beliefs, or Carmen. She believed that was the beauty of it, being able to have either opinion and to make your own choice.

Becky fell somewhere in the middle of Andrea and Carmen. She wanted to have a career, but she also wanted to spend time with her children and build a home for them—she just hadn't bargained to do all the work. She thought Kenny would help some, but he never had. She believed in the middle ground, that both husband and wife could work and share the responsibilities equally. What she believed didn't matter anymore. The court now set the responsibilities and the time and everything else. They made it joint custody. Too bad it wasn't 'joint' before the divorce.

Kenny's eyes and focus were looking down at the bowl of soup. "It shouldn't be like that, but sadly it's a lot of men's thinking when they get married, including mine at the time. I guess no one kicked my butt into the current century until now. I watched my father sit on his butt after he got home from work as my mother waited on him hand and foot. He was tired after a long day at the car factory. I guess in my father's defense, my mother didn't work."

"Didn't work? She ran the household like a well-oiled machine and she raised four boys," Becky said a little aggravated. This was the reason she left his sorry behind three years ago.

He seemed to realize his mistake in words and stumbled and stuttered, "I…I…mean…she didn't work a job…"

"A job? Isn't taking care of children a job? I know lots of women who don't work outside of the home, and the job they do is much harder than the job their husband's do when they're supposed to be working. Do they get coffee breaks? No. Lunch by themselves? No. Time to go to the bathroom in peace without children calling or hanging on them? No. Women who stay home work just as hard, if not harder than men who work and women who work and take care of the house and kids are purely amazing! They should get an award."

"I guess I didn't treat you like you were amazing enough, did I?" Kenny asked, his head hanging low like a dog that had been scolded.

This subject was making her uncomfortable. The past was the past. All this conversation was doing was reminding her of why they weren't married and why she left him in the first place—his conservative manly mentality and his lack of attention to her, the boys and their lives. It didn't matter that he was starting to see some of the errors of his ways. Did it? She took another swallow of the soup he spooned into her mouth.

She shook her head. "I'm full."

"Why don't you rest for a minute while I clean the kitchen? Then I'll help you to the bathroom and maybe even a sponge bath or shower, whatever you feel up to," Kenny proposed as he stood up with the half-eaten bowl of soup in his hands.

She swallowed the last bite of noodle in her mouth and almost choked on it. Sponge bath? Toilet? Shower? Becky wasn't at ease with this kind of thing while they'd been married, taking care of intimate matters in front of him. Now that they were divorced, she was down right petrified of the thought.

Becky let her gaze wander around the room. All of the roses he'd given her were decorating the tables and mantle, along with the other flowers from friends and family and the balloons from Justin and Adam. She swallowed back the emotion clogging her throat. She realized through this process she had a lot of good friends and family.

She glanced toward the kitchen where Kenny was busily scrubbing pans and studied him from under her long eyelashes. He certainly appeared to have changed quite a bit—not completely—but he was obviously working on things. Cooking classes and cleaning the kitchen were pretty good indications.

However, the memory of her always being mad at him

for setting his dishes in the sink instead of placing them in the dishwasher or leaving them in front of the television until she gave in to the mess and picked them up burned her throat. Becky exhaled the breath she was holding. She did need to use the bathroom. She supposed now was as good a time as any to jump over that hurdle.

"Um … Kenny?"

"Yes?" He looked up, bubbles covering his hands. He always had such long fingers and strong hands—a basketball player's hands. She couldn't help remembering how his fingers felt caressing her skin, the way they seemed to glide across her back, the way they lingered in her hair. She shook her head to clear away those kinds of thoughts.

"I need to use the bathroom," Becky said in a tentative voice as she tried to slide up on the cushion.

Her head felt like the wood a lumberjack split with an axe. She gritted her teeth with determination. The more she did for herself, the less Kenny had to help her with, she reasoned. She pushed to a standing position and locked her knees. Suddenly, she felt herself shaking like a small twig during a hurricane. Her jaw hurt from gritting her teeth so hard. She drew in a shaky breath and willed herself to stay upright. She wasn't going to fall. She wasn't going to fall. She *was* going to fall.

"Easy there!" Kenny scolded as he ran to her side just in time to catch her as her knees gave out and she fell forward.

"I can do it!" Becky barked in frustration.

"I know you can, but it would be a lot easier if you'd just let me help you. Your stubbornness is very cute and also very annoying."

"You never helped me before," she bit out in the midst of her pain. Becky didn't know which was worse… the pain in her heart or the pain in her head.

"I'm changing, Bec, I'm working on it. Let me prove it to you. Give me a chance. I know I'm not perfect. I might never be, but all I can do is try."

He gathered her gently in his arms and carried her to the bathroom. She had no choice other than to let him help her. She was too weak to protest and she really did have to go.

Her feet had barely touched the floor in front of the commode when her knees betrayed her yet again and she started to shake. The distance between her and the brown tile was shrinking. Becky reached out and grabbed Kenny by his green shirt. His arms automatically curled gently around her waist. If anyone were to walk in and see them, it would look like they were dancing.

Becky didn't know if she was breathless from the feel of his chest beneath her palms and his body so close or because she just had surgery. She said in between gulps of air, "I… my… pants…"

She attempted to pull them down, but nothing seemed to be working like it used to. Her entire body wasn't her own. What happened to the body that could take a basketball and shoot it from the three-point line for a swish? What happened to that body that could run five miles before even going to work a full day managing her companies? It seemed some alien or something had snatched her healthy and athletic body and gave her this feeble poor excuse of a shell.

"I can do it," Kenny said without hesitation. He reached between them and pushed down her pants and underwear, gently lowering her to sit on the toilet. Her cheeks turned a crimson color. She felt so mortified and vulnerable she dared not look at him. The same man that had seen her naked countless times and seen her give birth now made her self-conscious of her state of undress.

"Bec, I've seen you naked. I've held you in my arms and made love to you more times then I can count. I've even seen you give birth to our two sons. Why are you so embarrassed now?" It was as if he read her mind, or at least went down the same reason trail as her mind.

"If you must know, I'm uncomfortable because we're

no longer married. This type of intimacy is for people who are married... or at least in a relationship." She tried to empty her bladder, but she couldn't with him standing so close and holding on to her so she wouldn't fall over. "And to be honest, I didn't like taking care of my needs in front of you back when we were married. I like my privacy."

"We *are* in a relationship," he comforted. "We are friends. We are parents to our children."

"I can't go," she finally said.

Kenny reached over and turned on the faucet. "Maybe the sound of running water will help."

"Maybe you leaving and giving me some privacy will help much better."

"If I leave you alone, you will fall. You didn't even have enough strength to pull down your own pants. How do you expect to support your weight and sit there?" Kenny said as he put his hand under her chin and tilted her face to look at him.

She could feel her eyes watering, but she refused to let the tears fall. She was strong. She could do this. Becky grumbled, "Fine. Stand there."

Becky concentrated as hard as she could on the running water and finally said, "I'm done. Could you hand me some toilet paper?"

She heard the noise of the roll and soon felt paper in her left hand. "Thank you."

After she took care of everything, Kenny tugged her up, helping her to stand to straighten her pants and then wash her hands.

"Do you want to get a shower or bath while you're up?" Kenny offered.

She didn't even have to think about that question. "No."

There was no way she'd be able to get through having him see her completely naked while she bathed. This was hard enough to do the way it was.

"Well then, back to the couch." Kenny lifted her back into his arms and returned her to the sofa.

Eight

She spent the rest of the day sleeping and when she wasn't sleeping, Kenny would bring her more soup, pudding, and Jell-O. He even took her to the bathroom two more times. It still wasn't easy with him helping or watching, but he did his best to turn his head away and give her as much privacy as possible while holding on to her with his hands. And she did her best to pretend that he wasn't there listening.

She told him after the last trip, "I'm going to try to sit up for a few minutes. Maybe that will help me gain my strength back." She had to work her way up to taking care of herself and away from needing his help. The sooner she did, the better it would be all the way around.

"All right. Do you want to watch television or read?"

"No. How about we just talk?"

"That's fine with me. What do you want to talk about? The weather?" Kenny laughed playfully.

"Your work."

"My work?" Kenny seemed stunned. "You never liked hearing about my work before. I thought it bored you."

"No, it doesn't bore me. I guess the reason I didn't take much interest in it before was because I was usually resentful and mad at you all the time. I suppose I didn't make much of an effort to learn about your day or even if you were happy doing what you do," Becky admitted as she sat up on the couch. Her head was spinning, but she refused to give in to the carousel ride.

"I'm sorry I gave you reason to be resentful and mad at me all the time."

"I'm sorry, too. Sorry I wasn't adult enough to communicate my feelings better. I guess I never really appreciated what you did until now," Becky admitted. "Please tell me about your work. I'm listening now."

Kenny hesitated a second and then began talking about his job. Becky stilled and listened for the first time in years and actually heard what he was saying. So often he would tell her things and she'd listen with half an ear as she folded laundry, cooked or cleaned. She never really sat still long enough to listen to his every word and inflection before. It was strange how much you actually heard when you stayed quiet and paid attention.

"You seem to really love what you do," Becky stated softly and reached for his arm. "I think I need to lie down now."

Kenny aided her in lying down. She peered into his face and marveled how good age looked on him. She gave a small smile. "Thank you for today."

"You're welcome," Kenny said softly. She thought she saw a spark of something in his eyes, but he quickly stood up before she could be sure if she had and called over his shoulder, "Get some rest."

"Can I see the boys soon?" Becky asked as her eyes grew heavy and started to close.

"The doctor and everyone who loves you thought it best to give you peace and quiet for a few days before we let the craziness back in. I don't think you would take it easy knowing the boys were watching or needing you. Am I right?" Kenny asked.

"You're right. I probably would try not to look so sick and overdo it. Is Andrea okay with watching them?" Becky asked in a drowsy voice.

"She's happy to have them. I think Chloe is happy to have Justin around. I swear that one day those two are going to get married," Kenny mused as she started to glide into the darkness of sleep

"Maybe God will let me be around to see their wedding day…"

The sun was shining through the slits in the blinds when she woke the next morning. She looked at the clock on the mantle. Seven o'clock. She'd slept all night. However, as her body and consciousness woke, so did the pain. Becky slowly rotated her eyes to take a look around the room and found Kenny sleeping in a chair nearby. Sometimes, like this moment, his presence managed to warm her heart.

She needed to use the bathroom, but didn't want to wake him from his peaceful sleep. Becky managed to use the couch arm along with the table to push to her feet. When had sitting, standing and walking become so difficult? She shuffled her feet slowly and inch-by-inch made her way across the plush carpet to the powder room. It seemed like a feat close to climbing Mt. Everest.

Her hand finally rested on the six-panel door—almost to the top of the mountain. She made it to the toilet—the mountain's peak. She sighed. Using the bathroom was a major accomplishment now. Becky finished and while she was leaning against the sink washing her hands, she felt motivated and confident she could do more. She had walked on her own and managed to make it to the bathroom by taking it one step at a time. Maybe washing off in the sink wouldn't be so difficult after all, she thought as she stared at the running water. She was sure she wasn't smelling the greatest. It had been a while since her last sponge bath by a nurse in the hospital. Becky wanted to smell good for… Well… she just wanted to smell good.

Becky plugged the sink, let it fill with warm water and grabbed a washcloth off the rack. Picking up the bar of soap sitting in the crystal dish, she lathered it up and washed her face and her arms. The warm soapy bubbles felt so good and refreshing that she sighed. She decided to slip off her top and sponge completely off. Her grandmother often took baths in a sink in her later years. She'd told Becky that taking a bath in the bathtub was just too dangerous at her age and that it only spelled disaster or a broken hip. She was a spry woman who worked her fingers to the bone cleaning houses until she was eighty-two.

Her grandmother died a natural death with a smile on her face sitting in her favorite chair still living at her house. Becky hoped she had the privilege to make it through all of this and live as long and as full a life as her grandmother had done.

Pretty soon her entire upper torso was lathered with soap. Some might think it was a poor excuse for a shower or bath, although to her it felt heavenly. Days in the hospital and grime washed away.

She dipped the cloth into the tepid water and was about to rinse off the soap when the stripes on the wallpaper started to look like zebras running by. She swallowed hard and felt herself sway. She tried to reach for the pedestal sink, but the marble surface of the sink was slippery and her hands were slick with soap. Becky's fingers ended up slithering off the porcelain like they were grasping a greased pig.

A slight scream erupted from her throat and she felt her body slide downward to hit the floor with a thud—then nothing.

❀ ❀ ❀

"Becky?" Through a heavy fog she heard Kenny's voice call to her.

"Ummm..."

"Becky?" he called again.

"Yessss...."

"Are you all right?" he asked in concern, dabbing a cold washcloth on her forehead.

"I think so," she murmured in a daze then warily glanced around. She was on the floor of the bathroom, the tile cold against the bare skin of her back. "What...?"

"You must've become dizzy while giving yourself a sponge bath and collapsed. I heard you call my name. You were already on the floor when I found you," Kenny explained as he turned the cloth over and put it back on her head again.

Her head was hurting worse than before, but nothing seemed really overly wrong that some extra pain medicine wouldn't fix. Becky tried to sit up and moaned from the intensity of the pain.

Kenny lifted her easily in his arms. "Why don't I carry you to bed? You'll be more comfortable there and I can finish rinsing the soap off better where there's more space."

The words 'rinse the soap off' triggered her realization and memory of her exposure. Horrified by her nakedness, she stared down at her bare breasts still adorned with soap bubbles. Could this possibly get any worse? she groaned inwardly. She tried to use one hand to cover herself, but then found she couldn't hold on as well. Finally giving up, she closed her eyes, hoping she'd wake up to find it had all been a bad dream.

She felt the soft bed sag under her body as Kenny placed her on the king-sized bed. He turned around and disappeared into the bathroom, swiftly returning with a washcloth and bowl of warm water.

Becky looked on as he dipped the washcloth in the water, squeezed out the excess and slowly wiped the soap from her body. Her heartbeat felt like it was speeding faster than a racecar at the Daytona 500. After the initial shock she placed her hand over his and stopped the movement of the cloth.

"I can do it," she insisted in a quivering voice.

"All right. I'll hold the bowl," Kenny told her.

She continued the chore of rinsing away the soap, but couldn't help noticing the unstated electricity in the room. She felt like she was being zapped by it. What was the saying about being near water and lightning?

"Umm… I think… I think I'm done." Becky handed him back the cloth.

"What do you want to wear?" Kenny asked as he cleared his throat.

"I guess a big t-shirt." Becky suggested her usual attire, pointing toward the dresser.

Kenny nodded and moved over to open a drawer and sift through the contents. Her throat convulsed as she remembered what was in that drawer.

"Wait!" she yelled.

Just as the word 'wait' screamed from her throat, she noticed Kenny's expression change. The air seemed to disappear from the room as she lost her breath.

"I can explain… I…" Becky stuttered.

Kenny stood up with the t-shirt in his hand, staring down at it in confusion. It was one of his old t-shirts that he'd left behind. She had about three of them that he hadn't taken with him, plus the one he'd loaned her the other night for the sleepover at Carmen's house.

Becky was originally planning on giving them back or maybe even throwing them away to prove he was out of her life for good, to prove she didn't need him, but a small part of her couldn't do either. Instead, she'd put them in a drawer and found herself even wearing them at night sometimes—usually on the nights she was lonely or missed Kenny. They were comfortable and reminded her of him.

"You don't have to explain." He grabbed one and slipped it over her head. "But I wish I would've known you still had feelings for me before now. A lot of time and heartache could've been avoided."

"I don't know what you're talking about. I just kept them because they fit good." Becky told half of the truth. She had to save her pride, had to save face and herself from any more embarrassment.

"Bec, why can't you just admit there is something still between us?" Kenny asked as he shoved a hand through a lock of red hair on his forehead. She couldn't help noticing everything about him, from that dimple in his right cheek to the reddish brown shadow he always got when he failed to shave. The slight beard gave his youthful face a more mature and wise look.

"I'm tired and my head hurts. I'm going to go to sleep now. You can sleep in the boys' room if you want or the couch. Whatever is fine," Becky sidestepped the question.

"You win for now. Go to sleep." Kenny covered her up with a sheet, disappearing through the bedroom door.

Despite how exhausted she was, the turmoil of emotions kept her awake. Her mind kept going over the years she'd spent with Kenny. Finally, after many hours, she managed to fall into a restless slumber with images of her ex-husband floating around like sugarplums dancing in her head.

Becky was frustrated. She was excited to have company, however, that excitement was wearing off.

She pulled at Kenny's t-shirt, taking her frustration out on the cotton instead of her friend. "The doctor said I have several weeks to decide about chemotherapy. They believe all the tumor was removed, but follow up treatment is strongly advised. It's my body and ultimately the final decision is mine. And to be honest, I don't really want to feel sick. I don't have time to feel sick. I have two boys to raise and businesses to run."

"Becky, you aren't going to have anything to run or anyone to raise if you don't take care of yourself and agree to the treatment. I think it's pretty straightforward. I don't know why you even have to think about it. Get the treatment and then get on with your life. The chemotherapy will give you a life to get on to," Carmen insisted as she handed her best friend a cup of steaming hot tea. Becky preferred coffee but that was no longer on the menu.

"It's easy for you to say. You're not the one who's going to feel like you've been body slammed or have a horrible hang-over like we did in college all the time," Becky snipped back. She regretted how she sounded, but her nerves and temperament weren't quite the same lately.

"So what? You got drunk in college with no real reward—just to get drunk. You'll be feeling like dog poop now for a reason... saving your life." Carmen plopped down next to Becky on the bed, sloshing some of her own tea onto the creamy white sheets. Becky liked the color white. It was crisp, clean and orderly. She liked order.

"Oops, sorry," Carmen quipped with no real regret in her voice. "You need to stop living in your own little world and wake up. You had a brain tumor. You survived. You're sitting here alive and that is a blessing in itself. Stop worrying about what you might or might not feel like after your treatments. Just take them and keep focusing on your two boys and nothing else. It's that simple. This is a black and white decision."

"You're not the one who's going through this! It's easy for you to advise and recommend. I'm the one who just had surgery. I can't even go to the bathroom without Kenny helping me. I don't want to depend on him or anyone else any more. I want to get back to my normal old life. Chemo will only delay that and make me needy that much longer."

Becky's voice was rising like a high wind. She didn't care if Kenny heard her from the other room. She was tired of all this.

"Becky, you better get used to depending on your friends, and even Kenny who still loves you, I might add, and stop being 'Miss Independent' and 'Miss I Can Do Everything Myself.' You don't have to do everything yourself and you aren't alone. So stop thinking you can handle this without help! You can't and you don't have to," Carmen yelled right back. "I love you and I'm going to help your sorry butt whether your independent ego let's me or not! If you don't get that damn treatment you might die and I'm not ready to lose my best friend! Got that?"

Becky just sat staring at Carmen unable to say a word. She was stunned at her friend's emotional outburst. They looked at each other for a very long time. The clock ticking in the background sounded like a bomb marking its impending explosion. Was she the bomb or was Carmen?

At that moment, Kenny walked into the room holding a tray filled with food. "Lunch is ready. There's enough here for everyone."

Carmen mouth was drawn down into a tight line. "I'm not hungry. Good to see you again, Ken."

She gave him a nod as she strode out of the bedroom.

"What's got her all upset?"

"Nothing."

"It can't be nothing. I've seen you two butt heads over the years, but this seems more than nothing. Something's got her upset," Kenny commented as he brought the food to the bed.

The aroma smelled heavenly and looked great. There were several different sandwiches and fresh fruit.

"You remembered my favorites… turkey and cheese with pickles." Becky couldn't help but feel touched by his gesture, not only remembering what she liked but actually making it for her The old Kenny wasn't romantic or sensitive to her needs. This Kenny was different. Completely different.

"I remembered. How can I forget that you love everything with pickles?" Kenny teased. "I think you'd even eat lobster with pickles."

She took a bite and hummed in her throat. "Delicious. This is the first thing that has tasted good since my surgery, well, besides the chicken noodle soup yesterday."

"I'm glad. I was starting to worry. You didn't have any weight to lose before all this and to see you not eating and getting thinner... I had to think of something you would eat." Kenny bit into his own sandwich as he sat next to her on the edge of the bed.

They sat in perfect silence, neither wanting to break the bond that somehow had reformed between them. After every few nibbles, she'd sneak a glance from under her lashes to study his features. He'd changed so much, and sadly, the change had come too late. She wished he could've been like this while they were married. If he had been, they wouldn't be divorced now.

Kenny finished eating and took her plate. "Do you need anything else?"

"No, I'm fine. Well, maybe if you could just turn on the television before you go, please."

He flipped the TV on and handed her the remote. "Just yell if you want me."

She nodded, her eyes drifting to his cute bottom as he walked away. Just yell if she wanted him? Oh, she wanted him, but not in the way he meant. She scolded herself out loud, "Will you stop staring at his backside, for heaven's sake!"

Kenny leaned back into the room with a lopsided grin. "I don't mind."

Becky blushed furiously. He winked and disappeared again.

When Andrea came by the next day, Becky was sitting up. Her friend breezed into the bedroom with a plate of cookies and a handful of magazines.

"Hope you like reading about scandals. I bought all the juicy magazines I could find off the rack," Andrea grinned mischievously.

Becky was going to deny her love of reading about Hollywood actors and actresses but didn't because Andrea would know she was lying. She always enjoyed talking to Tammy Jane on the phone about the latest news since she lived and worked in the midst of it all.

"Thanks. Anything good?" Becky asked, taking the stack.

"Oh, the usual divorce and drug addiction stories," Andrea answered, plopping down on the bed, nearly landing on top of her best friend's legs. "I don't know why you love this smut anyway. It's not real life. It's not normal people's lives."

"Isn't it? I think we're not so different from them. The only thing that sets us apart is their lives and secrets are publicized and ours is not. They have problems just like us." Becky held up the cover of one magazine. "See the latest on a divorce. Well, if you haven't forgotten I'm divorced. And the other breaking news is an actress got caught not matching her handbag with her outfit. If they took a picture of me some mornings going to work... I'd be on the worst dressed list for sure." She laughed and added, "Especially now that I'm bald."

"So, are you a druggie too?" Andrea laughed as she pointed to the other headline about an actor going into rehab for drug use.

Becky waved her hand at the bottles on her side table. "I guess I am, but these don't make me feel good."

"Well, if you slip me a hundred, maybe I can buy you

some good weed," Andrea retorted, a twinkle of teasing in her eye.

"Very funny. Instead of weed, I'll just be happy with a good bath to make me feel better." Becky shook her head at her friend's humor. "I partially sponged off in the sink and let me tell you, I think I can smell myself."

"You know, now that you mention it, I saw a headline on one of those magazines about an actor who would show up at the gambling casinos stinking and obviously needing a bath. I guess you're right about them not being so different from us after all." Andrea tried to sound serious and was failing because of the giggles in her voice.

"Yeah, well, this is no casino."

Andrea became somber and offered, "If you want I can help you take a bath."

"Well…" Becky hesitated. It felt weird having her friend see her naked and help bathe her, however, the only other choice was her ex-husband. Besides, in the old days they'd seen each other undressed in locker rooms and all those sleepovers where they didn't care about undressing in front of each other. She might be older now and not as perky, but she was desperate. "All right. I guess. If you don't mind?"

"I don't mind. I'll just treat you like I would Chloe when she was little. I'll start the water and you get undressed," Andrea ordered in a stern, no-nonsense voice.

Becky sighed. She wasn't a child. Sickness had its degrading moments. The image of using the bathroom with Kenny standing next to her popped into her head as one of them.

Andrea came back from the master bath a few minutes later and slipped a hand under her friend's arm. "Bath time, Missy. And I can't stress how much you need one."

"I think you just told me I stink." Becky stared down at her petite friend.

"Yeah, well, it's the hard core truth. You smell like a

mixture between hospital disinfectant and the locker rooms in high school."

"Gee, don't sugarcoat it." Becky couldn't help a small chuckle.

Andrea soon had her friend in a warm, soothing bubble bath. She helped Becky scrub her back. Her friend joked from her kneeling position next to the tub, "You remind me of Chloe, just with less hair and bigger boobs."

Becky felt a twinge in her gut from the less hair comment. Andrea must've realized she stuck her foot in her mouth for she quickly added with tears in her eyes, "I'm sorry. That didn't come out right."

"Don't be. I feel like I belong in a freak show."

"You're not a freak. You look like the kids back in high school who shaved their heads to make a statement about being different. It's all right to be different." Andrea placed a soapy hand on her friend's shoulder. "It's odd that back then, to be honest, I thought they were freaks. Now that I'm older and wiser, I realize they were just showing all of us with prejudices that we shouldn't judge by appearance. They were wise beyond their years. They knew at a much younger age that it was okay to be different."

"If different means sitting in a bathtub naked and hairless as a baby's bottom, having my best friend bathe me because I'm too weak from having surgery and having my ex-husband wait on me and take me potty like one of the kids… then I guess I succeeded in being *different*. Oh, and for the record, I'm not completely like those kids in high school. I didn't choose to shave my head."

Andrea was quiet for a second before continuing in a soothing voice, "You're right. You didn't choose. What's happening to you stinks. But you can either wallow in your own pity or be wise like those teenagers with bald heads and show that it's cool to be different. And furthermore, you might want to get your wise butt to the doctor and start those treatments and get on with your life for Justin and

Adam's sake. What's it going to be? Are you going to roll over and die or beat this thing?"

Becky's shoulder's drooped from the weight of the last couple of weeks. "I can tell you've been talking to Carmen behind my back."

"We both love you. It wasn't done in gossip. It was done in love. She was worried about you, that's all. She loves you like I love you. We're all sisters."

"Well, sister, neither one of you has mentioned anything to Kenny, have you? Becky asked with a touch of a worried edge in her tone. "I don't want him to know I was thinking of not taking the chemo treatments."

"Nope. But if you don't take the chemo, I think he's going to figure it out on his own. He's not dumb, you know," Andrea stated firmly and then asked again, "You still haven't answered, what it's going to be? Are you going to roll over and die or beat this thing?"

Becky looked at the pictures of Adam and Justin sitting on the stand next to her perfume bottle. "I'm going to beat this thing," Becky said in an uncertain soft tone.

"What are you going to do?" Andrea said a little louder.

"I'm going to beat this thing," Becky repeated.

"One more time!" Her friend moved her arm cheerleader fashion.

"Okay, stop the cheerleading pep talk. I bet you'd never think you would go from what team are we going to beat to what disease are we going to beat?" Becky said with sarcasm.

"Hey, life is full of things we have to beat… and if you don't start acting like the tough athlete who can score twenty and thirty points in a basketball game, then I'm going to kick you in the…"

Andrea didn't get a chance to say the last word because Kenny knocked on the doorframe and strode into the bathroom. He asked with a raised eyebrow, "What's all the yelling about in here? Is everything okay?"

"I'm just helping Becky with her bath and was planning on giving her a good swift kick in the..." Andrea was cut off again but this time by her friend.

"Okay. Okay. Kenny gets the picture," Becky muttered, getting a little nervous about her ex-husband standing in the room with nothing between her and his admiring eyes except a froth of bubbles.

"Since you're here, why don't you help me get Becky out of the tub? She's looking a tad pale. I'd hate for her to take a fall. I think I let her soak a little too long."

"Sure, no problem." Kenny moved over to stand near Andrea by the tub.

"I can do it," Becky said stubbornly.

"You don't want to collapse and knock your head again, do you?" Kenny reminded with concern.

"We both know you can do it, but you look awfully pale, and why take the chance of breaking a bone to add to your recovery time?" Andrea pointed out reasonably.

Becky could've sworn there was a twinkle of mischief in Andrea's eye. The same twinkle she had the time she and Carmen jumped on the Ferris wheel and left Becky with Kenny—the age-old twinkle of matchmaking in progress.

"Fine." Becky gave in yet again. So much for independence and the ability to say no.

Kenny lifted her out of the tub with no difficulty and stood her on the bath rug. Then Andrea wrapped her friend in a huge fuzzy white towel. She was scooped up in her ex-husband's arms and carried back to the bed. She had to admit she felt a little dizzy and a part of her was thankful Kenny was there to help, but she wasn't about to admit it to either of them.

"I'll leave Andrea to help you finish getting cleaned up," Kenny said, shifting from side to side, looking a little nervous.

"Thanks, Kenny," Andrea called after him as he

quickly left the room. She smiled at her friend, beaming. "Let's make you look like a queen."

"I don't think that's possible," Becky said, running a hand over her smooth head.

"Anything's possible," Andrea informed her as she hurried into the bathroom and brought back an armload of beauty supplies. "Anything is possible."

Becky was thankful that she had such good friends like Andrea and Carmen, feeling a little bad that Carmen had walked out yesterday in a huff.

"I don't usually wear much makeup," Becky protested. She was a tomboy by nature. Wearing makeup and making sure she had the right purse to match her outfit wasn't something she normally took time to consider or cared to do.

Andrea opened up a compact and told her, "Look into the mirror and tell me again you don't need makeup."

Becky gazed at the reflection staring back at her. The long flowing black hair that looked like ink being poured down a waterfall was completely gone. The full red lips Carmen had joked she was jealous of because Becky didn't need any lipstick. Those lips that used to be full and the color of a red apple, now were cracked and split open like a dry desert.

At one time her eyes were as clear as if you were looking into a mountain stream down to the brown dirt floor bed at the bottom. However, even though the brown color didn't change, there was a sadness that muddied that sparkling clearness.

"A little blush here, a touch of lipstick here…" Andrea talked as she worked, "Well, today you're going to wear more makeup. To be honest, you need more right now. Your face is the color of that white pillowcase behind you and your lips look wrinkled and dehydrated," Andrea said as she began painting her friend's nails a bright red color.

"I'm going to look like I belong on Hooker Street."

Becky rolled her big brown eyes.

"Well, if that helps you get back together with Kenny, then Hooker Street isn't so bad," Andrea snickered as she sprayed some perfume on Becky's neck.

"Gotcha! You *are* trying to set Kenny and me back up!"

"Hey, I never denied trying. I think you were stupid for divorcing the man in the first place. How many times have I told you that? So, he wasn't romantic or much help around the house. So he forgot special occasions and was gone being a kid a lot. He was a good guy and had great potential. You just needed to train him better," Andrea grinned, "A good whip, maybe?"

"Andrea!" Becky admonished, getting her double meaning. "I thought homemakers were supposed to be quiet and reserved."

"I think the world is full of discriminations. People assume that a homemaker is quiet and dull and we're not. People assume that a person with their head shaved is a freak and they're not," Andrea defended and added, "For the record, I believe in doing whatever you feel comfortable with to spice up a marriage and keep it together. If that means a whip and you both are okay with that then bring out the whip. Maybe if people stopped being so concerned with what others think then more marriages would stay together and there would be less divorce. Communication and acceptance is the key."

Becky shook her head. "I'm not sure if that's too much information about the whip thing or if it's just the right amount to help me realize that if I don't want to be judged, I shouldn't judge others."

"Exactly." Andrea nodded toward the compact mirror still in Becky's hands. "Did I do a good job?"

"You did a fine job," Becky said in a tone that hid any turmoil. "A fine job indeed." What she said was true. Andrea did a great job for what she had to work with.

"I'll call Kenny in to show him the new you," Andrea

announced with glee.

"I'm sure he's busy." Desperately, Becky tried to redirect her friend.

"Not too busy for someone as gorgeous as you," Andrea said with enthusiasm. 'I'll tell him to come up on my way out."

"Tell the boys that I miss them. I hope you can bring them back later today," Becky said in anticipation of seeing her children again. "I feel much better and thanks to you, now I look much better as well. I won't look so scary to them since you performed your cosmetic miracle."

"I left them with my hubby while I came to visit you. They're having a great time playing with their godfather." Andrea nodded and flipped her hair. "Besides, I wanted to make sure you were ready before I brought them to see you. And now that you're bathed and cleaned up, I think you just might be ready."

"I'm more than ready. I miss them terribly. I can't wait to have them here and all to myself."

"I imagine if Kenny stays here with you, the boys shouldn't be too much to handle," Andrea commented in a firm tone.

"Kenny stay here with me?" Becky stated in confusion.

"Bec, you haven't even been able to stand on your own two feet yet without falling over. Granted, you do look better after your bath and visiting 'Andrea's Beauty Salon,' but don't fool yourself into thinking you can take care of two active boys, cook and watch out for them. I'm sure Kenny will stay. I'll mention it to him on my way out as well. Now, I'm off to find that hunk of an ex-husband of yours. Tootles." Andrea gave Becky a quick hug and then rushed out the door yelling for Kenny.

Becky's mind and heart were racing. What would the boys say about Kenny staying with her? What would Kenny think of her all fixed up? Her heart was beating as fast as hummingbird's wings. Her body shuddered with unwanted emotion. Andrea did her magic and what she had to work with was great, but it still couldn't hide what the body went through.

She heard footsteps in the hall. When Kenny stopped in the doorway, Becky felt her throat tighten. She sat waiting for his inspection and response. It seemed to take forever for him to speak. "Andrea was right, you look beautiful."

She patted the rainbow scarf that Andrea had put on her head. "Andrea decided I needed a pick-me-up."

"Well, I guess then a pick-me-up you shall get!" Kenny grinned slyly and walked over and gathered her in his arms. Their gazes drifted to each other and locked. Kenny slowly lowered his head toward hers, brushing his warm lips over hers lightly in a feathery touch. At first, she thought she was just dreaming the kiss, but when she opened her eyes just slightly she realized it was all too real.

Her eyes fluttered closed again and she felt herself giving in to his kiss, the past years just washing away like dirt in the rain. It felt like their first kiss. His tongue teased the insides of her mouth. The wall she'd erected for protection against this very thing was crumbling, the reasons she had for leaving him fading like an old photograph. All she felt was his kiss and the burning feeling inside.

She pushed against his chest and said breathlessly, "I can't."

"You can. I know you want to. I can feel the passion you have for me under the surface. Just give in…" Kenny murmured as his lips found hers again.

Becky's mind went foggy with passion. She groaned and felt herself melting against him. She didn't know if it was the weakness from her surgery or the weakness from the buried feelings she had for him resurfacing. The clock chimed where it sat on the mantle of the bedroom fireplace. It was like a wake up call to her senses. She pushed against his chest yet again to come up for air, struggling to find the inner strength to fight against what she really wanted. "I can't and I won't. Please put me down. The boys are coming back today… we can't confuse them like this…"

Kenny held her for a moment longer, almost as if trying to decide what to do. He finally moved over to the bed and placed her on top of it. He turned on his heels and strode out the door without looking back or saying another word.

Nine

Becky forced herself to call down for Kenny. When he came up to the room he was acting normal enough. Maybe he'd forgotten all about the kiss already. She certainly had not.

"Can you carry me downstairs?" Becky forced herself to ask his help. It about killed her to do so. She didn't want to be in his arms again, remembering the heated kiss from the last time he'd held her in a warm embrace.

"Sure," Kenny answered tonelessly.

He picked her off the bed and carried her down the stairs and placed her on the couch without another romantic incident. She had to admit, a part of her was sad about that, wanting for an instant to have it happen again. She quickly buried that part. How much more mixed-up could she get?

"Andrea mentioned that she talked to you about me helping out while you're recovering. Are you sure you're all right with me staying here until after you're done with your chemotherapy and back on your feet?"

"Until after my chemo?" Becky stated in shock. When she'd talked with Andrea earlier, she thought the idea was for Kenny to be staying until she was stronger and not finished with her chemotherapy treatments.

"Wasn't that what you decided?" Kenny asked, a little confused from the stunned expression on Becky's face. "Andrea told me as she was leaving she thought the boys would be too much for you to handle while you're dealing with recovering from the surgery and then recovering from the treatments. She was worried about you and about their safety if anything would happen to you."

"Until after my chemo is fine," Becky answered in defeat. "Besides, do I really have a choice? I might be stubborn and pigheaded, but I'm not stupid. I don't want you here taking care of me, however, I know that if I collapse or get sick that I put Adam and Justin in danger and I would never do that. I also know if I let you keep the boys while I go through chemo, I'll be heartbroken not seeing them. They're what keep me going and it's hard enough going a few days without seeing them when it's your time. So, I guess like I said... do I have a choice?"

"You always have a choice. I'm glad though, that you're looking at it realistically for the boys' sake. It's only for a short time and we'll all manage to get through it and back to normal in no time," Kenny said with a smile, "besides, you make it sound like a horrible fate having to be around me for a while."

She smiled despite her irritation. "Not a horrible fate. Maybe just a terrible fate."

The room filled with unspoken emotions for a second and then cleared when the boys came bursting through the door holding gifts for their mother.

"What beautiful cards and flowers!" Becky exclaimed as Justin and Adam tackled her with hugs, nearly knocking her over with enthusiasm to see her. The pain shot through her head and into her body. She started to feel queasy from the throbbing.

"Boys! Be gentle with your mother. She's still recovering from surgery," Kenny scolded as he came over and sat down next to Becky on the couch. He put his arm around her. The boys nodded that they heard their father and then a grin came over their boyish faces.

Becky knew what they were thinking. They saw their dad with a protective arm around their mother and it was like a happy ending to a movie or their wishes coming true. She cleared her throat and asked Kenny, "Would you mind putting these gorgeous flowers in water for me?" She had to get him away from her.

"Sure," Kenny smiled, not realizing her ploy worked.

"Where did you get such beautiful flowers?" Becky tried to get Justin and Adam's mind off of their matchmaking schemes and on to something else.

"We picked them from Aunt Andrea's garden. Did you know she has an entire garden that she uses to cook all the meals with?" Justin said in awe.

"I know. She loves gardening and flowers." Becky smiled at her sons. Andrea chose to stay home rather than pursue her original goal of opening up her very own floral shop. Her friend had a creative gift. Her makeover earlier today was proof of her abilities.

"Did you two behave at Aunt Andrea's house?" Kenny asked with a raised eyebrow.

"We did. Although Justin spent all of his time playing with Chloe and forgot about me." Adam taunted his brother with an elbow to the ribs.

Kenny and Becky looked at each other trying hard to hide their smiles. Young love was so innocent. It was old love that made things so complicated and tainted. She wished she could still see Kenny through the same eyes she had when she was just thirteen. The kind of eyes that didn't see any faults but saw everything in a sunny light.

"Where are we going tonight? Aunt Andrea just dropped us off. Are we going back with her again or staying with Mom or going home with you, Dad? I'm confused on who gets us today," Justin commented as he ran over to the television to turn on cartoons.

The solitude of the past few days was replaced by a beautiful noisiness. She'd missed the sweet chaos that kids provided. The kind of mess that took your mind off things like cancer and recovery.

"Well, actually, for a little while we both get you," Kenny told them with a cheerful smile. "While your mother is going through getting a special medical treatment called chemotherapy, I'm going to stay here helping her out with you guys."

"That means we're going to be a family again?" Justin asked, a rush of tears springing to his eyes as he flung a quick glance over his shoulder, for a moment forgetting about the cartoons. He was always the sensitive one, which was probably why Chloe liked him. He had the biggest heart.

"Well, not exactly. We're all going to live together for a short time until Mommy can get completely better, then things will go back to the way they were," Becky tried to explain.

"We want things to go back the way they were a long time ago like in the pictures when we were little. You and Daddy hugging and we were a big happy family," Justin said, his lashes wet with tears.

Becky knew he'd always been very sensitive to the divorce, but she hadn't realized until this moment how upset he really was. She used all her strength to push off the couch and hobble over to Justin by the television and kiss him on the forehead. "Mommy and Daddy both love you and we'll always love you whether we're together or not."

She could tell Kenny was concerned about her walking unaided, but surprisingly he let her. Maybe he realized how important it was that the boys see her in a positive healthier light.

"I love you too, Mom." Justin smiled up at her. Becky was starting to feel a little shaky. She looked back at Kenny. He must've sensed her need for he came over and put his arm casually around her waist, giving her support without being too obvious.

"Your mother and I both love you," Kenny said firmly.

Adam snorted in response to that statement. She could tell Adam was about to lose his composure. His little ears almost matched his hair. Kenny must've seen his reaction for he quickly guided the boys away from the emotional subject. "How about a game of catch in the backyard?"

Justin immediately yelped, "Yeah!"

Adam paused a second as if thinking whether or not he wanted to throw a fit or throw a ball. He decided on the ball and Becky was relieved. "Sounds fine."

"Go get your mitts out of the laundry room," Kenny instructed. Adam and Justin ran out of the room to find their baseball gloves.

"Let's get you back to the couch to rest," Kenny said in a whisper.

She sighed and leaned against his body for support. "Thank you."

The past few weeks had been so emotionally draining. Becky wondered if the path she'd chosen three years ago had been the right one. Right now it seemed that God had other plans for her and those plans all seemed to be diverging onto a path that had Kenny's name all over it.

"You're welcome." Kenny kissed the top of her head quickly and then walked out of the room to go play ball with his kids—something he'd rarely done before the divorce.

Becky sighed again. She looked at the kitchen. Perseverance. She pushed up on feeble legs. Life was too short to spend it sitting on this blasted couch. She managed to hold on to things and make her way to the kitchen and found what she was looking for.

She struggled to pick up the glass pitcher to make lemonade. The carafe felt like the hundred pound weight she used to be able to pump easily at the gym. Now a one pound glass pitcher felt incredibly heavy. Becky took a deep breath and clunked it on top of the granite countertop. Thankfully it didn't break. After about ten minutes, she was stirring the liquid and the ice together. She knew she needed to sit down, her legs were shaky and her hands trembled.

She fell heavily into a kitchen chair with a sigh and a groan. In the past she could make lemonade in two minutes or faster and at the same time be chopping fresh fruit. She scolded herself out loud, "Now look at you. You can't even make a pitcher of lemonade for your family."

"Family?" Kenny's voice spoke from behind her.

She didn't know what to say. She just bowed her head in defeat. He moved over to where she stood and rested a hand on her shoulder. "You need to stop living in the past, but instead live in today. Yes, in the past you could do lots of things but this isn't the past, it's the here and now. Stop comparing apples to oranges, or in this case to lemons. You're going to have to work your way back. Maybe you'll never be as strong as before or maybe you'll be even stronger. But stop worrying about what was and concentrate on what is."

Kenny sounded so wise and his wisdom was so frustrating. She knew he was right, however, it didn't change the fact that it stunk—royally.

"I made lemonade for you guys." Becky pointed toward the counter where the lemonade was waiting ready to be consumed. Pointing was all she could do, she didn't have the strength to carry it out back for them.

Kenney picked up the pitcher and glasses and carried them outside to the picnic table. When he returned, he scooped her up in his arms and carried her out as well.

"So, I guess this is my new method of transportation?" Becky teased, trying to lighten the mood.

"It sure has less pollution than a car," Kenny chuckled, "and hopefully cuter."

She blushed, felt the heat curl across her cheeks. "I guess cuter."

Adam came rushing up for the cool drink and added, "Yes, but Dad has his own method of polluting the air, he toots a lot!" Giggling, Adam ran off again with the cup of liquid sloshing over the rim and onto the grass.

Becky burst out laughing at her son's reference to gaseous body noises and Kenny. Her ex-husband acted offended and then joined in the laughter. "I guess I can't deny that remark."

Justin grabbed his lemonade, putting in his two-cents worth. "Nope. You're the king of gas, Dad."

"Thanks, Justin old boy. I'm glad you think I'm a king of something!" Kenny called after him as rushed back to his brother.

"They're your boys."

"Yep, they sure are. And I'm proud of them."

The next couple of days went smoothly for having her ex-husband in the same house again. The boys seemed to feed on the fact they were all together and it had been a long time since she'd seen them this happy. Justin and Adam wore huge grins on their faces no matter what. They even carried out the trash without complaining, their eyes sparkling and grins wide as they did the smelly chore they usually hated doing.

Kenny commented, "Don't you think it's a little odd how chipper they are while taking out the garbage?"

She nodded. "I sure do. However, I'm not complaining about it. Usually I get whines and 'I'll do it later's.' It's nice to see them like this."

"Yeah, it is nice."

"I think they really want us back together," Becky said before thinking.

"I do too," Kenny agreed as he dusted a piece of furniture.

"Is that why you're cleaning, cooking and pampering

me?" she asked with an eyebrow raised.

"Is it working?" His grin was lopsided.

"I'd be lying if I said it wasn't. I know I wasn't keen on you being here, but I couldn't get through this on my own. Without you."

"When do you start chemo?"

"Tomorrow. I start it tomorrow, which is frustrating. I'm just now getting some of my strength back. I can actually sit up and walk without falling over like a baby taking his first steps."

"Bec, I'm glad you've decided to take the chemotherapy."

"Why wouldn't I be taking the chemo?" she asked, surprised at his comment. Did Andrea and Carmen tell him that she was considering not doing it? If they did she was going to be mad as hell.

"I could see it in your eyes when the doctor was telling you about it. I could tell you were considering not going through with it."

She knew she looked guilty. Becky admitted, "You're right. I wasn't going to do it. Between Carmen harping on me and Andrea guilting me into it, I decided it was the right thing to do for Justin and Adam's sake. I owe it to the kids to do what I have to do to get better. I'd die to save them so I figured it should work the same way in that I would live for them."

"Everything will be just fine."

"You don't know that. Nobody but God knows that," Becky said in a matter-a-fact voice. "Speaking of knowing, if you knew I was leaning in the direction of not doing the treatments, why didn't you try to talk me into it like everyone else?" A part of her was sad that he didn't care enough to insist she do. Maybe she was misreading all the signals she thought were loud and clear until now.

Kenny shook his head in dismay. "Who says I didn't try?"

"What?" She didn't understand.

"I did try. You just didn't see me try. I talked to Carmen and I talked to Andrea. They were my first lines of offense. I was going to be the last line of attack," Kenny claimed, a please-don't-be-mad-at-me look on his features.

"I see. So you went behind my back and talked to my friends and had them talk to me?" Becky summed it up.

"Are you mad?" Kenny now looked worried.

"No, I'm not mad. To be honest, I thought for a second you didn't care enough to try. I'm glad you still care." Before she thought of what she was doing, she raised her hand to run it through her hair but realized she had none. Old habits were hard to break. Instead, she adjusted the scarf encasing her head.

"I care, Bec. I care more than you'll ever know. I love you," Kenny said and somehow over their discussion, he'd moved closer and was right in front of her.

"Kenny..."

"I want you back in my life, more than just an arrangement like this. I want you back as my wife again."

She knew he was going to kiss her, knew she had to do something. She sidestepped his attempt and threw her hand up to stop him. "We can't."

"Why not? I love you. I want to make love to you." Kenny took another step toward her.

"We're not married."

"I love you, Becky, I haven't kissed another woman since you. And that excuse is getting old, we both still wear our wedding rings. I call that married even if the state doesn't recognize it. I know my heart still recognizes it and so does God."

He hadn't kissed another woman in three years? What about that girlfriend he was referring to the other day. She thought there was someone serious in his life now or at some point over the years. It was hard for her to believe there wasn't.

"Nothing changes the fact that we're divorced," she

protested, trying to reason with him. Although, she wasn't sure who she was trying to convince. Kenny or herself.

He lifted her left hand and held it up for her to see. "We are married, Becky." He touched her chest over her heart and then her head. "We're married in here and in here where it counts. I don't need a piece of paper to tell me that. Do you?"

"I can't do this, Kenny. I need to focus my energy on getting better and starting chemo. I don't have the capacity to figure all of this out and to complicate matters more by pursuing what might or might not be between us."

Adam yelled from upstairs. "Dad! Justin is bothering me!"

Kenny was going to say something else she could tell, but he closed his mouth and instead called out, "Coming, boys?"

Ten

Tomorrow became today too quickly. She was sitting in the car more frightened than she could ever imagine. The last twenty-four hours had flown by. She thought she had time to adjust to this idea, but she wasn't ready. She wasn't ready to begin this part of the journey, yet she didn't really have a choice. She meant what she said about loving Adam and Justin too much not to take this giant step. Becky had many friends over the years that had faced this disease, either themselves or with parents, grandparents, relatives, or sadly, their children.

She was glad she was facing this road and not her children. Why were children always so much braver? she wondered. Her friend Eileen had a son who had gone through the debilitating illness associated with cancer and you couldn't wipe the smile and determination from little his face. He was the sweetest and bravest little boy… who now was in high school, healthy and dating some girl. Why did it seem like such a huge mountain to climb for her when someone four times as young could climb it, not only with perseverance, but with a smile?

Becky supposed anger and pity got in the way of most adults that children didn't really take on. Adults usually got mad at God and then threw a pity party for themselves... like she found herself doing so often.

"Are you ready?" Kenny asked as they pulled away from the curb in his truck.

"Do I have a choice?" Becky blurted out before she had a chance to bite her tongue.

"You do. You have a choice whether to sit and sulk or take this as a challenge you're going to win. So, what's it going to be? Are you in the starting lineup or are you sitting on the bench not even in the game?" her ex-husband asked with a sideways look.

She took a long moment to think about that. It wasn't a game, but he was right. She had a choice whether to join in and fight with her body or just roll over and die. "I'm in the game."

"Good. Now start acting like it." Kenny reached across the space between them and tweaked her nose.

"You know, I'm starting not to like you again," she stated in a mocking voice. Her joke fell flat yet again.

"I thought I told you to stop making jokes when you're nervous. You stink at them." Kenny shook his finger at her as if she were an errant child.

"You're right. It's a habit I have yet to break."

"I think they have shock collars for habits like that, where I just push a button and you get zapped." Kenny smiled teasingly. "I heard some people use them to train animals."

"I'll remember that when I need to zap you for something like forgetting the dishes or overlooking that stack of laundry in the middle of the floor," Becky countered.

"Does that mean we're getting married again?" Kenny asked hopefully, one eyebrow raised. "Because those certainly sound like married fighting words."

"I...I..." Becky stuttered and thankfully was saved from answering as they pulled up to the hospital.

"Today is the first day of the rest of your life. Get your

butt into that hospital and let's win this!" Kenny playfully tapped her on the bottom.

She jumped from the love tap and gave him a dirty look before she turned back around. When her face wasn't in his view anymore, she grinned.

The wait was long. When they were finally called in to see the doctor, Becky's heart was racing. Now she understood what a panic attack felt like. It almost seemed like her heart was going to explode out of her chest from the strain.

"So, Becky, how are you feeling today?" the doctor asked.

"I'm fine. I'm fine enough not to have to do this. See, a complete miracle. I feel healed," Becky said as she jumped off the patient table and twirled around and around.

"I see that. However, I'd like to make sure we eradicated all the cancer, so I'd like to go ahead with the chemo treatments even though you're cured. You'll probably feel tired, fatigued and could lose your hair in the process."

"I guess the hair loss shouldn't be an issue," Becky said resentfully as she touched her rainbow-covered head.

"Yes, for you it shouldn't be a problem. Now that we got that subject taken care of, why don't I send you over to begin your first round of treatments?" the doctor said with a kind smile. "Any questions?"

"The only question I have is if the chemo is going to guarantee that I will see my children's weddings?" Becky asked, knowing full well there was no guarantee for anything.

"Years ago, having cancer was a death sentence. We've come a long way to providing patients in your situation a chance at a long life," the doctor told her as he pushed his glasses into place. "But as you know, there are no guarantees in life."

"Sorry. I know. I'm grateful. I'm just scared."

Kenny took her hand. "You're not alone. Come on, let's get you started on your drugs."

"Great. Now, I'm a drug addict." Becky couldn't help

trying to lighten the moment with one of her jokes again.

"At least these drugs are mostly covered by insurance," the doctor teased back.

"Do they allow me to see rainbows and purple pigs?" she asked.

"Nope, but they do give you the ability to appreciate life, which is a gift in itself," the doctor said in a voice no longer bantering.

She nodded, knowing he was right about that. Some great gifts came in ugly boxes. This ugly box was cancer with her name on the receiving end, but the gift inside was the appreciation of life and the ability to see things and people differently. She saw Kenny differently now. She saw her own children differently. Becky realized that every day was a gift and that folding laundry, going to the bathroom by herself, having her body working and strong, sitting on a hard bleacher while watching her children play sports, and a husband that loved her, even though he had faults, was a blessing indeed.

The next several weeks seemed to fly by. She received her treatments on schedule. After the completion of each treatment, she felt weak and sick just like the doctor warned. She'd usually fall asleep on the couch while watching television and later found herself tucked cozily in bed. At first she was embarrassed by the gesture from Kenny, however, as the weeks went on, she was thankful for everything he did.

It seemed like she fell asleep at the strangest times. She'd be watching Justin and Adam play baseball, her head would droop and she'd wake up with her head resting on Kenny's shoulder several innings later. He no longer sat on the opposite side of the field. He was always right next to her, making sure she was all right. It was actually nice and reassuring knowing that moments like those wouldn't affect her children's safety. If she didn't have Kenny there, she didn't know what would happen. What if she fell asleep and someone took the boys? Or what if she fell asleep and something bad happened? Having someone by her side gave her the freedom and luxury to give in to those moments of fatigue with the knowledge that someone reliable had her back.

Kenny wasn't the only one looking out for her. Carmen would hand her bottles of water to keep her hydrated and Andrea always had peppermints in her pockets for when a bout of nausea would overtake her and she had to run to the bathroom to lose the contents of her stomach. Justin and Adam seemed to be by her side holding her hand whenever possible. It brought tears to her eyes to have such compassion and support from those who cared about her.

"Bec, why don't we go shopping?" Carmen asked her one day as they were sitting at a baseball game watching Blake, Justin and Adam play.

"Shopping?" Becky asked in surprise. "What brought on the need to spend money?" Usually Carmen spent money when she was upset or fighting with her husband. They loved each other but Carmen loved to fight. Carmen had that tendency to fight with those she loved. It was just her argumentative nature. Becky believed it was because she felt comfortable enough to express her feelings passionately.

"No reason," Carmen answered, shrugging her petite shoulders.

"Are you and your hubby fighting again about the in-laws?" Becky asked suspiciously. Her friend often complained about the in-laws and how they liked to tell her how to raise Blake.

"Nope."

"You didn't have a car accident again, did you?" she prompted, remembering one occasion Carmen wanted to go shopping after she wrecked her car. She was putting lipstick on while driving. Thankfully no one was hurt, but her husband had been angry over the incident.

"No, everything's fine." Carmen waved her hand dismissively.

"Spill it. You never want to shop unless something is wrong. We spent all of our time shopping in high school because of guy problems and all of our adult lives so far shopping because of marriage problems. You haven't a piece of clothing in your wardrobe that couldn't tell a story about how and why it was bought," Becky remarked smartly, giving her friend a knowing look.

"Fine. You've got me. I want to shop because I'm cheating on my husband."

"What?" Becky exclaimed, almost falling out of her seat.

"I'm just joking. If you need a reason for us to shop, I can make one up if you like," Carmen said giving her this 'I won look.'

"Fine. If there isn't a reason, I believe you. When do you want to go on this shopping spree of yours?"

"How about in two weeks? That will be your last chemo treatment so we can celebrate. How's that sound to you? We can go out to eat and then shop till we…" Carmen stopped her words.

"You don't have to always be careful of what you say. It's okay," Becky told her best friend. "You can say 'drop.' I won't be offended or break into tears."

"Sounds great. We'll shop till we drop."

"Good. I'll see you at noon at our usual eating trough in two weeks." Becky said as the game ended. The score was ten to four in favor of the boys' team.

"Great. Noon in two weeks sounds good."

"What about noon in two weeks?" Kenny walked up carrying four snow cones.

"Carmen and I are going out to lunch before I go in for my last chemo treatment. Make it as fun of a day as possible. Why four this time, Ken?" Becky asked in surprise as she stared at the treat in his hands.

"One for Blake, Justin, Adam and, of course, one for my lady," Kenny told her, handing her one. "Remember, you need to keep yourself hydrated. You've been spending most of your time in the bathroom lately. I'm starting to think you have a thing for the porcelain throne."

"Hey, don't knock it. I'm starting to like the graffiti on the walls in the public bathrooms. Did you know that Jim loves Kim?" Becky teased.

"I do now," Kenny laughed.

Becky took a bite of the flavored ice. It actually tasted really good on her tongue. She was starting to appreciate what it was like to be a kid again and enjoy things like snow cones.

"Mom, do you feel up to going out to eat at the pizza place?" Justin asked, with such hope in his eyes it was hard to deny him. She didn't know if she could stomach the smell of pizza, but the plea on his sweet face was one she just couldn't resist.

"Sure. I feel up to anything with you boys." She pasted a smile on her features, hoping she sounded more confident that she felt.

"Great! Let's go." Justin pulled on his mom's arm.

"Have a good time," Carmen called after them with that impish twinkle in her eye. Becky knew that look all too well, knew what her friend was thinking and she was thinking the same thing. They seemed like a family again.

This time they headed for the same vehicle without asking. There was no begging to ride together or the awkwardness of whose time it was with the kids. She nearly laughed at the memory of the other pizza place outing. She had been too stubborn to go into Kenny's truck, and yet, now he took her everywhere.

Kenny helped her into the seat and closed the door. She watched him out of the corner of her eye. Could a zebra change their stripes and even if he didn't, did she love him for the unique stripes he had?

"Pizza with our usual pepperoni sounds awesome." Adam clapped his hands together in excitement. Becky's stomach churned at the thought of the heavy aroma she was going to have to endure. She put a hand across her abdomen to comfort the body part.

Kenny cast a sympathetic look her way and reached over to hold her hand. She didn't pull away. She allowed him to hold it—as much for herself as for him.

At the restaurant, the waitress remembered them, ushering them to the same booth they had before. Kenny and Becky sat next to each other yet again. She laughed silently at how life circled around sometimes. They placed their order, Justin and Adam chattering on like monkeys. She just smiled and listened to all their tales.

The waitress served their pizza and set it down in front of her. Becky felt her stomach churn at the smell. She knew it wouldn't be long until she'd have to make a made dash to the rest room. She immediately nudged Kenny. "Excuse me."

Kenny quickly hopped out and let her by. Becky rushed to the lady's bathroom like she had before, however, this time she actually had a reason. She flew into the stall, marveling at the irony of the situation. Last time, she sat on the filthy floor, oblivious and uncaring of how dirty it was, and now she was hugging the toilet to keep herself from falling over, not caring, or able to care, about how unbelievable unsanitary it was.

She heard a familiar voice. "Bec?"

"In the last stall," she called as her head began to spin and she got sick all over again.

Becky felt a hand on her shoulder and knew Kenny was standing behind her. A cool paper towel swathed the back of her neck. She sighed. She never liked throwing up. Becky supposed no one did, but it was one of the things that rated right up there with getting a gynecology exam or a root canal.

After the nausea subsided, she turned her gaze toward Kenny. He took another paper towel and wiped her face and around her mouth. She gave him an appreciative look.

"Do you have a stash of wet wipes in your pocket?" Becky teased weakly.

"No, I just yanked two out of the holder and wet them as I passed by. I knew you'd be needing them." Kenny looked around the lady's bathroom. "This sadly has become our meeting spot."

"Yes, people are going to start thinking we're together again if we keep this up."

"Becky, we need to work on that habit of yours of saying things when you're nervous or upset. You have great jokes otherwise." Kenny smiled and touched her cheek with the back of his hand.

"Sorry, it's a hard habit to break, but people are going to think we're together." Becky took a deep breath trying to regain her strength.

"Is that so bad?"

She shook her head. "No, that wouldn't be so bad."

Kenny smiled with relief. "For a moment, I thought you were going to say it was."

Becky replied in a weary voice, "How about we take this date out of this fine establishment of a bathroom."

"Deal." Kenny stood up and offered her his arm. "Shall we?"

She took it for support. "Let's." They started for the door and Becky paused a step at the sink. "I need to wash my hands first if you don't mind."

"I think I'll join you." Their eyes met in the mirror.

"So, what do you think of the lady's restroom?" Becky chuckled.

"I remember sneaking into the girl's bathroom when I was a kid trying to see what made them so different and more special than the boy's bathroom."

"What did you decide was so special?" Becky inquired, studying him as he washed his long strong fingers.

"I decided your bathroom was usually cleaner, didn't have the urinals like we did, and had metal boxes I just didn't understand." He pointed to the feminine hygiene dispensing machine on the wall.

"That's all right. When I snuck into the boy's bathroom, I didn't understand how you could pee standing up with someone watching you. I still don't get that." She chuckled, remembering how uncomfortable she was with Kenny helping her go to the bathroom after her surgery.

"You just get used to it," Kenny explained.

"I guess so." She lifted a shoulder in a slight shrug. "It wasn't so horrible after a couple of times with you helping me to the bathroom, but I can't say I'd like doing it all the time."

Kenny took her arm again and they walked out arm in arm. The same lady was seated near the bathroom entrance they'd seen before. She gasped when Becky and Kenny walked by her. She gave them a strange look and remarked. "Again?"

Becky tried to stifle her giggles and Kenny smiled. "Sorry. Hopefully, this is the last time I have to use the lady's room." He added jokingly, "It's that darn long line at the men's room."

Kenny and Becky tried to restrain themselves. When they returned to their table, they burst into fits of laughter. Justin asked, "What's so funny?"

"Life. Life is good, son." Kenny laughed and kissed Becky on the cheek.

Adam smiled because everyone else was smiling. "I love my family."

"Me too," Justin agreed as he dug into another slice of pizza. Becky watched, amazed at his appetite for someone so slender.

"Me three," Kenny piped in, picking up a slice of

pizza. Becky watched her family eat and managed to nibble on a breadstick.

Eleven

Thank goodness, her last round of chemotherapy was nearly over. Carmen was sitting with her eating lunch at McDonalds. Her friend flicked a brown strand of hair out of her eyes and asked, "What's on your mind?"

"I'm just wondering, what now?"

"What do you mean what now?" Carmen looked confused as she bit into her cheeseburger. Becky only sipped a soda.

"Well, I've focused all my energy and thoughts on one thing only and that was getting through the treatments. Today is my last treatment and I'm asking myself, now what?" Becky explained as she ran a hand over the rainbow scarf on her head. It was her standard accessory.

"You go on living your life," Carmen stated.

"What life? I'm not sure the life I was living was the one that I want to go back to." She straightened the scarf and smoothed down her baggy shirt. All of her clothes were shapeless now that she'd lost so much weight.

"I never understood why you didn't get a wig," her friend bluntly declared as she dipped a greasy fry into blob of ketchup.

"I just didn't feel the need. I guess I realized through all of this how I look to society is not that important. What *is* important is how I feel about myself. I'm all right with my scarf. I have no one to impress anyway."

"Not even Kenny?" Carmen challenged. "You don't want to look good for your ex-husband who you've gotten quite chummy with lately?"

"It's not like that. We're just friends. We share a common bond and that bond is Justin and Adam, that's all." Becky felt a rise of frustration with the direction the conversation was going. The memory of Andrea putting makeup on her came to mind and Kenny's kiss that came afterwards.

"I don't think it's friendship I'm seeing in Kenny's eyes and you're fooling yourself if you think there's just friendship in your own," Carmen argued as she took a sip of her diet soda filled with caffeine.

"We're not together like that."

"Maybe if you put on a wig, you might be. If you're not careful, you could lose that ex of yours to a woman like that big-chested leopard-bikini bimbo," Carmen avowed and then put her hand up to her mouth. "I'm so sorry."

"Carmen, I love you. I love that you feel comfortable enough to share your mind with me, but you need to be careful of what you say. For the record, Kenny isn't like that. He likes a person for who they are inside and not because of their hair or their big boobs. If he likes me, and I say *if*, then it wouldn't be because of my long black hair or lack thereof."

"I just mean that you should try to spark things up a little between you two. I read a book once that said even though the man likes you for what's in your heart, it's nice to dress up the package sometimes," Carmen said as she wiped ketchup off her freckled cheek.

"You know what I like about McDonalds?" Becky asked, changing the subject to a more comfortable topic.

"What? You didn't eat a thing, so it can't be the food."

"No, the food's just fine when I'm not battling cancer and my stomach isn't queasy," Becky clarified.

"Speaking of food, you really need to try to eat more. You're getting so thin."

"I would if I could. They tried to give me something to alleviate my nausea, but nothing they tried worked. I take comfort in the fact that today is my last treatment and I'm done." Becky took another drink of her lonely soda.

"So, you never finished your sentence. What do you really like about McDonalds?" Carmen reminded her of the original topic.

"Sorry, lately my mind wanders and I go off on a tangent. What I really like about McDonald's is that it's busy with different types of people. It's like the melting pot of society. You have the young, the old, the rich, the poor, the scholarly type, the artist, the posh business man, the secretary, the injured, and the bald like me. Everyone is acceptable and everyone comes in this place," Becky commented as she removed her scarf exposing her shimmering smooth scalp.

"I suppose. The food's good and a lot of people eat here," Carmen said as she glanced around the room. "It's turned out to be quite a profitable business, and speaking of businesses, how's yours doing?"

"Better if I could be there. I need to get my work hours back to the usual sixty a week. I've only been able to work barely fifteen hours during this time. The chemo has exhausted me, drained me of energy and I barely have anything left to even think about work."

"You just need to let go and hire someone to manage your companies for you then you wouldn't have to worry about how many hours you work or getting everything up to speed. There's got to be someone you trust to do that job," Carmen said as she stood to smooth her pleated khaki pants.

"No, if that was the case, then I would've done it by now. My companies are like my babies. I hate to see them in someone else's hands, especially a stranger's." Becky stood up as well, straightening her own clothing.

"They aren't your babies. They're just things. Your children and Kenny are what should matter the most. I thought you learned that much through all of this." Carmen spoke her mind yet again. Her friend's way of thinking sometimes hurt.

"I've learned how important it all is and I've always thought it was, but…" Becky tried to defend herself.

"But what?" Carmen raised a shapely brown eyebrow. "There are no buts, only just truths." Her friend kissed her cheek and waved goodbye and was out in a blur of designer clothes.

Becky stared after her brazen friend. She had to admit Carmen was right most of the time in what she said—most of the time. She walked out of the restaurant and headed to the hospital.

Kenny swung her around in a complete circle, celebrating the last chemo treatment. "You're done! Today was your last one!"

"I think I'm going to be sick," Becky said, growing dizzy from being spun so fast.

He quickly set her feet back on the ground and had the decency to have a sheepish look cross his features. "I'm so sorry for getting carried away."

"I'm fine. The dizziness is fading." She did her best to give him a reassuring smile.

"Why don't we go pick the boys up from school and do something fun?"

"Like what?"

"There's a fair in town. We can take the boys with us. I saw the announcement in the paper about it."

She shrugged. "I guess that sounds fine. I usually feel

worse the day after my chemo. I still have a few good hours in me before I start hugging the porcelain throne again."

"Good. It's settled. We'll go gorge ourselves on fair food and watch the boys ride all the rides. It'll be a blast."

They picked the boys up from school, surprising them with the idea of spending an afternoon of fun together. Adam shrieked in excitement, "Way cool!"

Justin smiled in anticipation. "I've never been to a fair. It sounds like fun."

Becky and Kenny exchanged stunned glances. She asked in astonishment, "We've never taken you to a fair?"

"Nope," Justin answered promptly.

"Well, you're going to the fair today," Kenny said firmly and grinned. "All kids need to go to a fair sometime in their lives. You haven't experienced life until you eat huge pickles and funnel cakes."

It wasn't long before they pulled up into the fairground parking lot. Kenny took his usual place by her side as they walked up to a booth and bought tickets. Everything looked vaguely familiar. Her footsteps slowed, and she hesitated, however, she didn't have a chance to think about it because Adam dragged her forward.

"Easy, son. Be gentle with your mother," Kenny admonished in a stern voice.

"Sorry, Mom," Adam apologized as he loosened his hold. "I'm just so excited to…"

Justin interrupted, giving Adam an elbow in the ribs and finished his brother's sentence. "He's just so excited to see all the rides."

Adam pulled them all toward the amusement park rides, dragging them into a long line. She found herself at the Ferris wheel, struck with a feeling of déjà vu. She forced herself to swallow.

"Something wrong?" Kenny asked, standing closely behind her.

"No, nothing is wrong." She was lying. Everything was

wrong. She was in line to the Ferris wheel. Again. The very ride where she and Kenny had met decades ago.

Becky was standing next to Adam and Kenny was standing next to Justin. At least she wouldn't have to ride with Kenny. The last thing she needed right now was to get emotional about a memory that was years and years in the past.

A tattoo-covered worker motioned them forward. She noticed he had a spider web covering his hand and an alligator on his face that opened and closed its mouth as the man spoke. It couldn't be? Could it?

"Move it!" he yelled. Justin jumped in front, grabbing Adam's hand and darted into the seat. Justin pulled down the bar with a click and told the ride attendant, "Bring us up."

Before Becky could tell him no, the carnival worker slid the bar forward and sent them upward. Damn. Now, she was standing next to Kenny and all the old memories came flooding back and hit her smack in the face like a boxer's glove. Thwack!

"Shall we?" Kenny motioned toward the empty seat waiting for them now.

"Get moving, people!" the man snarled. She had to laugh at the irony of the situation. What were the chances that Kenny would see the exact fair they'd gone to years earlier in the paper and take her to it? What were the chances they'd be on the same ride where they'd met and fell in love?

Becky sighed, "I guess."

They moved forward and climbed into the seat. The seats felt even smaller now that they were adults instead of thirteen year old kids. She glanced up at her children in the seat above them and blinked. Justin was grinning ear to ear and so was Adam. They reminded her of Carmen, Andrea and Tammy Jane all those years ago. Her eyes narrowed. She and Kenny had been duped.

"I think we were set up by our sneaky children." Becky pointed to the giggling pair.

"It appears so."

"How did you find out about this fair?" Becky asked with curiosity.

"The paper. It was lying on the kitchen counter open to upcoming events and I remember Justin telling me this morning that Blake mentioned a fair being in town."

"Oh really?" She shook her head in disbelief. "Blake mentioned it, did he?"

"I don't know. The idea just stuck in my head all day."

"I think Carmen probably told Blake about the fair and they schemed with Justin and Adam. I think our own children and my best friend pulled another fast one on us. What is that saying about fool me twice?" Becky laughed out loud.

"You think they went through all the trouble to get us here?"

"I know so. Those little matchmaking hooligans." Becky shook her finger at the snickering instigators. "I think Carmen told them how we met and they planned for us to get together again and…"

"Fall in love?" Kenny finished the sentence.

"I…"

She felt her breath come quickly as Kenny's lips claimed hers. His tongue tickled the inside of her mouth with quick movements. This time the dizziness had nothing to do with chemotherapy.

Becky pushed against Kenny's chest. "We can't."

"Why not?"

"Because our children are watching." She pointed to the two grinning boys.

"Let them see how much we love each other," he said as he leaned forward again.

She moved her head away so his lips wouldn't touch hers. "Kenny."

"I won't apologize. I should've kissed you like this the first time we met on this ride. I was too chicken then to take the chance. I'm not about to make that mistake twice. Life is too short and when you know how you feel about someone…"

"Kenny…" Becky said with tears in her eyes. "I…"

He took her hand in his. "It's all right, Bec. I know this probably isn't the time to discuss our future or our feelings. This is a time to just enjoy and be happy that today was your last chemotherapy. The future can wait."

She smiled her gratitude. "Thank you."

"You're welcome. But I have to say that your friends are nothing but determined to get us together and so are our children. I don't think we stand a chance fighting them on this, so we might as well give in." Kenny leaned over and kissed her cheek.

Kenny was right. Carmen was very headstrong. She usually got her way. It also just dawned on her why her friend had to go shopping. She was probably upset about sneaking around planning this get-together for the fair and her matchmaking attempt behind her back and had to take the guilt out on shopping. Becky had known something was going on with the hurried shopping trip. Now that she knew what, however, the more she thought about it, the more she was sure she wouldn't put Carmen on silent probation like when they were kids. Her friend was only doing what she thought was best.

Was it really best, though? She examined Kenny's happy face. For that one moment in time, life was crystal clear. She loved him. She wanted to be with him. Becky touched her covered head, sadness piercing her heart. It wasn't right for her to be with Kenny. He deserved someone he could fall in love with, someone he'd have better odds of growing old with. He deserved better. She had to let him go…

❀ ❀ ❀

Kenny was in the kitchen stirring a spoon in a big silver mixing bowl. "What are you making?" Becky asked, looking at what he was doing through curious eyes.

"A cake. I thought we should celebrate." He licked the spoon and offered it to her.

"A cake sounds yummy, but celebrating doesn't count until I'm officially cancer-free for five years. I don't think two months after the chemo is equivalent to five years."

"I think you should just forget about the five year mark and live day-to-day. I'm celebrating that you're up and around and not falling asleep on the couch, in the lawn chair, or missing work. I think those are excellent reasons to celebrate, don't you?" Kenny asked with an arch to one reddish eyebrow.

"I guess so," Becky hesitated before adding, "Speaking of all those things..."

"Yeah?"

"I think I'm back to my normal routine and... well, uh... I don't need any extra help anymore.... so..." Becky kept stuttering. How should she bring up the subject that it was best that he move out? She'd put off this day now for two months. The time never seemed right, still didn't. The selfish part of her wanted him to stay.

"Whatever you're trying to say, just say it."

"I'm trying to say that it's probably best that you move out now. The boys are going to get more and more attached to this situation the longer you stay and now there's no reason for you to stay... well... I think you probably should go... for the boys' sake." Becky fidgeted from side to side. The other reason he should move back out was that she was the one becoming more and more attached to the situation.

"I see."

"We're not married. We shouldn't be living together like this when there's no real reason. Justin and Adam will only get their feelings hurt more the longer they think we're a family again." She hoped her voice sounded firm.

"I see."

"Is that all you can say?" Becky asked, irritation spiking her voice.

"What do you want me to say? I won't beg you. If you don't want me in your life for more than an ex-husband, then there's nothing I can do about that." With Kenny's growing anger, he mixed the batter with hard intensity.

"I think the batter is blended." She motioned toward the goop in the bowl.

"I guess you know what's best—what's best about everything," Kenny murmured, his mouth drawn down into a tight line. He turned his back and worked on pouring the cake batter into the pan.

"I'm sorry, Kenny."

"So am I."

Twelve

She stretched her neck muscles from side to side. She was now back at the company working sixty hours again. Kenny had moved out and into his own place. Life seemed to go on just like before. However, now when she stopped for a moment to look around the house something was missing. It felt emptier without Kenny there.

Becky returned to working long hours when she didn't have the boys and taking care of them by herself when she did have them. The schedule reverted back to my time and your time again. It returned to the fast pace that it was before she was diagnosed. She was sure Carmen would lecture her about not learning anything from her ordeal. This thought haunted her work days and forced her to attempt to find a manager.

Becky tried to interview a few potential managers for the job of running the pharmacies, but no one panned out like she'd hoped. One lady was nice enough, but Becky could tell she was high on something and it wasn't life. Sadly, with a warehouse filled with drugs, you had to be careful who you trusted with them. She wished someone was as trustworthy as Carmen, Andrea or Tammy Jane.

❀ ❀ ❀

Becky was eating chicken with Justin and Adam one evening when Adam asked, "So, Mom, are you going on vacation with us like you promised?"

"I promised?" Becky asked, a small frown between her brows as she thought back until she remembered having the conversation at the pizza parlor right after she had her MRI. "If I remember correctly, I said I'd try and trying is different then promising."

"You said you'd try to find someone to help at work so you could come. Have you been looking for someone to fill in for you?" Justin probed.

"I… well… I've been busy. I've done some interviewing, though," Becky backtracked, with a touch of guilt.

"Being busy is no excuse," Adam said, his hands planted on his hips and his teal eyes blazing. He had his father's red hair and eyes.

"Careful with your tone, young man," Becky said firmly but gently.

"Sorry, Mom. I just want you to go so bad. I miss you and Dad being together. It was nice being like a normal family for that short time," Adam said, the look on his face like a puppy who'd been scolded.

I know. I'm sorry. I'll try harder to find someone to fill in for me. Is that good enough?" Becky said, tousling his hair.

"I guess," Adam answered with a grin and then added, "Isn't Chloe coming over soon?"

"Yes, soon," Becky answered, looking at the clock.

"Hey, Justin, your girlfriend is coming over soon!" Adam teased his brother as he put his napkin on his plate.

"She's not my girlfriend. We're just friends," Justin protested, his cheeks turning the color of his brother's hair.

"Uh-huh, sure you are." Adam jumped to his feet and danced around his brother.

"It seems like both of you have finished eating, so why don't you take your dishes to the sink and go outside and play?"

The boys did as she asked and right after the backdoor banged shut with a loud thud, the doorbell rang. It was Andrea standing at the door with Chloe.

"Where's Justin?" Chloe asked, peeking into the room.

Becky had to hide a smile. "Out back playing with Adam. Why don't you go join them? I think they're playing soccer."

Chloe streaked through the house and out the back door. Becky smiled at Andrea. "I think those two are going to end up being married one day."

Andrea grinned. "Justin is a good kid."

"Want a glass of wine?" Becky asked her friend.

"Sure, if you have red."

"I do. I have lots of wine since I haven't been able to touch it for a while. Come sit down and relax."

Becky poured a glass of red wine and handed it to her and Andrea commented as she sipped, "You don't look happy any more."

"Any more?"

"You looked so happy over the past few months." Andrea spoke softly, a touch of sympathy in her voice.

"I looked happy throwing up the entire contents of my stomach, losing my hair, shrinking two dress sizes, and not being able to walk around the house without needing to sit in a chair from fatigue?" Becky declared in disbelief.

"Yes, that's what I'm saying. I know you went through hell these past months on that kind of level, and I know it sounds weird saying this but you were happier than I've ever seen you."

"You're crazy."

"I'm not crazy. I think you're the one who's crazy for not realizing you're crazy in love again, and now that Kenny's no longer in your life, you miss him. You look worse now than you did battling cancer. Those bags under your eyes are just one example of what I'm talking about," Andrea said as she reached out and touched her hand.

"You're starting to sound like Carmen." Becky voice rang with rising anger.

"I guess I am. I just know that life is short and sometimes people need to hear things they don't want to hear for their own good." Andrea smiled kindly at her friend.

"In love?"

"Yes, in love. I don't think you've ever fallen out of love with Kenny, but now you've fallen into a deeper kind of love you probably didn't even know was possible. A love that embodies every sense of the marriage vows… through sickness and health…"

"It's funny how when you're married you say your vows without truly understanding them. You say them when you're young and healthy and at the top of the world. You think you're invincible and life is just going to be one giant vase full of roses," Becky admitted, and then her mind went back to the roses that Kenny gave her—life and roses.

"Then you figure out that life contains sickness, and valleys and even sadly sometimes poverty and death. Those vows seem to take on an entirely different meaning," Andrea finished. "You see your marriage vows and your promise to each other through more wise and experienced eyes."

"It's scary." Becky stared down at the empty finger on her left hand. She'd taken off her wedding ring the day Kenny packed up his things and left the second time around. She told herself she'd removed it because it was too big due to the weight she'd lost. Maybe the real reason she took it off was that she finally realized there was no hope for her and Kenny. She needed to let him go for his sake. No man deserved a sick woman hanging onto him, especially when the marriage vows no longer applied.

"Yes, it's scary depending on someone and being vulnerable with someone. When my mother died of breast cancer, I watched my dad suffer horribly through it all… through her radiation treatment and as she slipped away from us into the next life. I wasn't sure I ever wanted to have that kind of love my parents felt. The kind of love that when one suffers the other suffers, and when one dies, a part of the other dies. I swore after my mother passed away, I'd never get married… and then I fell in love and realized it was worth the risk of heartache like my father went through to experience the pure joy of loving someone so much." Andrea's hand wandered over her own heart.

"Andrea, I'm scared to let Kenny love me again. He doesn't deserve to be hurt if I die."

"Becky, my dad tells me to this day, he wouldn't trade a minute of his time with my mother. The time he had with her was the happiest of his life. Why are you denying Kenny that kind of happiness?"

"What if Kenny doesn't feel that loving me is worth it if he loses me?" Becky said, tears swimming in her eyes.

"I'm sure Kenny is petrified. He has the constant fear of losing you in the back of his head, yet it's so obvious he's willing to face those fears to have a chance at happiness and pure joy with you again."

"How do you know?" Becky challenged.

"He told me so," Andrea said staring Becky straight in the eyes. "He told me so the day I held him in the waiting room while you were in surgery. He cried in my arms, not because he might lose you, but because he might lose you before he had a chance to show you how much he loves you."

"I just finished my treatment and I can get sick again at any time. The usual big date is five years before all of this is declared 'officially' behind me, but I don't think it's ever officially behind anyone that goes through cancer. Even if doctors say that five years is the magical mark of being cured, I would imagine it's probably always in the back of your mind. I can't do that to Kenny. It's bad enough that I have to deal with it," Becky said, a tinge of sadness in her voice.

"Kenny is going to have to *deal* with it as you say, regardless of whether he loves you. Even though you're not officially in a relationship or married on paper any more, I know he considers himself married to you, the ring he leaves on and the look on his face is proof. So, apart from you taking him back, his connection to you is strong and he won't be spared if you get sick again. I'm sorry to have to tell you that. None of us will be spared. Not Justin, not Adam, not Kenny, or me, Carmen or Tammy Jane. Everyone who loves you will go through it and that's all right because loving you is worth the pain we'll suffer if we lose you. You're forgetting that anyone can die or get sick at any minute of the day. Life is about risk. If you don't risk—there is no reward."

"I know, but I guess it just seems more real that it will be me, given my current situation."

"Honey, anything and everything is real. I can die in a car accident tomorrow. It's all real… and what else is real is Kenny's love for you. Stop this pity party and get on with your life. You do have a life, you know. Start living it." Andrea stared down at her as she sat her empty glass on the counter.

"I made up my mind, I won't remarry Kenny. It's just not fair to him," Becky repeated firmly and gave her friend a hug. "Now, tell me about Chloe and that husband of yours."

"Nice change of subject." Andrea shook a finger at her friend and answered, "Well, the other day…"

Becky did as she promised and tried to find a replacement for herself so she could work less hours again and maybe even go on vacation with the boys and Kenny. She wasn't sure that was what she wanted, but she had to live up to the promise she'd made to her boys. She interviewed and hired a man who seemed nice enough, but caught him making a horrible joke to another worker about Jewish people. Becky fired him. She wanted nothing to do with discrimination in the workplace. She sighed. Good workers were hard to find.

The first thing Adam asked when she saw him was, "Did you hire someone yet?"

"No, son, I didn't. I'm trying." Becky gave him a lopsided grin.

"I hope you aren't just saying that and it's just a cover for not wanting to be around Dad," Adam challenged. She was taken aback by his audacity and also his keen perception.

"Well, I guess part of me doesn't want to go because your dad and I are divorced and it would be uncomfortable," Becky admitted, wanting to be honest as possible.

"You spent months together while you were sick and recovering. How's a vacation any different?" Adam asked, with innocence of a child.

"It's different because when I was sick I needed him and he was being kind to help me. If we went on vacation together, it would be for an entirely different reason and I'm not sure that's such a good idea." Becky touched Adam's shoulder, hoping to stem any further objections.

"Chloe said you should just get remarried and be done with it," Justin put in as he came into the room, catching the conversation.

"Oh, she did, did she?" Becky asked, slightly amused and slightly concerned they were discussing them.

"She did. She said you and Daddy belong together just like her and I belong together." Justin kicked at the carpeting with his foot.

"You and Chloe belong to each other?" Becky asked, trying not to smile or say anything to downplay their childlike feelings for each other.

"Yep, one day we'll get married, you'll see and one

day you and Dad will get remarried," Justin said with confidence.

"I think you two should go get washed up for dinner, that's what I think." Becky shooed them toward the bathroom.

"Awe, Mom, we aren't dirty." Adam held up filthy palms for her inspection.

"Nope, I see no dirt at all," she teased. "Get in there and scrub up. It's obvious you were digging for worms to go fishing again, weren't you?"

"Dad said he'd take us fishing tomorrow morning if that was all right with you," Adam admitted.

Becky paused. It was her time with the boys. She was about to say that she'd planned on taking them to the zoo, but couldn't say the words because of the excitement in their eyes.

"It's fine with me," she said instead.

"Great! Fishing with the entire family," Justin said as he skipped out of the room to wash his hands.

The entire family? What had she just agreed to?

The doorbell rang at six in the morning. Becky pattered down the stairs in her pajamas, wondering who was disturbing her at this hour. She peeked out the window and saw Kenny with fishing poles in his hands.

Becky swung the door open. "Kenny?"

"Didn't the boys tell you we were going fishing?" Kenny asked apologetically.

"Um, they did, but I didn't realize it was going to be this early." She tugged on Kenny's t-shirt she'd been using as a nightshirt self-consciously.

"You've got to catch fish when it's early," he explained, looking a little uneasy himself.

"Come on in. I'll make us some coffee while the boys are getting ready."

"Are you sure?"

"Of course. Why wouldn't I be sure?"

"Because before you got sick, you'd never think of letting me in, and after I moved back out when your treatment was finished, I got the impression that it went back to the way it was," Kenny admitted honestly.

"Oh. I'm not exactly sure what to say to that. I guess the best thing would be to say I'm sorry." Becky started a pot of coffee, keeping herself turned away.

"You shouldn't be sorry for how you feel."

"But that's not how I feel... not really," Becky confessed, glancing over her shoulder.

"How do you feel, then?" Kenny asked, propping a hand under his chin.

"I feel confused, that's how I feel. It's like a habit. I've somehow fallen back into the same ways as I had before I was diagnosed. I wanted things to be different." Becky ran a hand over her head, feeling the sleek strands under her fingertips. Her hair was growing back, coming in curlier then before.

"It's your life. If you want things to be different then it's up to you to make them different."

He made it sound so simple.

"I want to go back to that feeling that everything is special... every sunrise is a gift. It seems like I'm right back into that rat race I was in before, a race I don't want to be in."

"Then don't," Kenny stated.

"What about my businesses? What about my cancer? What about..."

"Becky, it's your life," Kenny repeated. "You can sell your companies. You've already won the battle against the cancer. You still need to make sure it doesn't attack again, but you've won. Haven't you learned to just follow your heart? What's your heart telling you?"

"My heart is telling me to..." Becky was about to say to love him, but Justin and Adam came running in the room all dressed and ready to fish.

"Hi, Dad! Fishing time." Justin jumped into his father's arms.

Kenny smiled at both boys. "That it is. Are you ready?"

"Let's go catch a big one." Adam grabbed one of the poles out of Kenny's hands then turned toward his mother. "Are you coming, Mom?"

"Me? Fish?" Becky didn't know how to answer that.

"Yes, you fish," Adam said grinning. "Girls do fish, you know."

"I know girls fish. Girls can do whatever they want," Becky said as she pinched his nose.

"Well, are you a girl or a fish?" Justin asked his mother, a challenge in his brown eyes.

"I'm a girl," Becky affirmed, a fist in the air.

"Then let's go." Kenny grinned and motioned for her to follow.

Becky glanced down at her clothes. "I've got to get dressed first."

"Just throw on a pair of old jeans or shorts and let's go catch some fish," Kenny told her as he carried both boys and poles in his arms. He had amazing strength.

"I'll be down in a jiff." Getting ready didn't take her long now-a-days. She didn't have to style her hair.

They went fishing and Becky couldn't remember ever having so much fun as a family. She laughed at Kenny's silly jokes and at Justin's attempt to bait a worm on his hook. He was such a sensitive kid. He tried to put the worm on as humanly as possible. Adam just stuck the worm on and was done. Justin, on the other hand, was so careful.

"Mom, I have an idea," Justin announced as he cast his line into the water.

"What's your idea?" Becky concentrated on the surface of the water, waiting for a fish to bite her hook.

"I think you should ask Aunt Carmen to run your companies."

"What?" Becky turned her head to stare at her son.

"Aunt Carmen. I think she should run your companies. Isn't that what she does for a living? Blake says his mom helps run a big company and she's important. Why not ask her?"

"Well…" Becky thought about that for a second. Why *not* ask her best friend? If she trusted Carmen with her most precious gifts in all of life—her boys—then trusting her friend with her companies should be simple.

"What do you think about my idea?"

"I think it's a good idea, but I'm not sure Aunt Carmen would want to give up her job. She likes her job."

Becky reeled in her line and looked at her hook. The hook was empty. The worm gone.

"I think you lost your worm." Adam hurried over to where she and Justin were fishing.

"I think I did."

"Let me put another one on for you, Mom," he offered.

"Thanks, Adam." She smiled with relief. She hated putting on the worms just like Justin did.

The afternoon proved to be as enjoyable as the morning. When Kenny dropped Becky off at home later, he walked her to the door.

"Thanks for letting me crash in on your time with the kids," he said as he stood next to her, waiting. She wasn't sure what he was waiting for.

She raised her hand and gently wiped dirt from his cheek. "You have worm dirt on your face."

"Thank you." Kenny caught her hand in midair, wanting to brush a kiss across her palm.

She sensed the undercurrent, strong as a river. She swallowed hard on the emotion, forcing herself not to give in to the impossible. "The boys are in the house."

"It never stopped us when we were married."

"The key word here is were," Becky pointed out. "We no longer are."

"Yes, you seem to keep reminding me of that fact."

"I think you should go now." Becky nodded toward his truck.

"I think I should." Kenny stood for a minute more, then turned on his muddy heel and walked away.

Becky knew she'd just pushed him away yet again, but knew it was the best thing, the only thing to do. She closed the door and her heart.

Thirteen

The insistent ringing of the phone woke her up from a deep sleep. She'd been dreaming about walking with Kenny on the beach, holding hands. She grumbled and rolled over to answer, "Hello?"

"Becky?"

"Yes?" she snapped in irritation. Who else would be answering the phone?

"It's Mom. I was checking on you, seeing how you were doing."

She cleared her throat and tried to fix her voice to sound more cheery. "Fine, Mom. Why the phone call so early?"

"I just miss you. I wish you would've let me come to be with you through all of your trouble. If Dad couldn't make it, I could've come anyway and taken care of you. My little girl is more important than anything else in the world." Her mother's voice was tight with emotion. Becky knew she was close to tears.

"I'm fine, Mom. There really wasn't anything you could've done anyway. Andrea watched the kids for me when needed and Kenny helped me out here. With your bad back, there wasn't much you could do. I'm way too heavy,"

Becky soothed. Her mother had back problems and the doctor had told her she shouldn't lift more than five pounds. Well, she definitely weighed more than five pounds and she really wanted her mother to be with her father. His needs far outweighed hers.

"But..."

"No, buts. Hopefully, this ordeal is behind us now." Becky decided now was a good time to change the topic of conversation. "How's the weather in old Florida?"

"Sunny," her mother answered, hesitated a moment, then added, "Kenny mentioned a long time ago that you might be coming next week to visit for vacation to our neck of the beach. Is that still on?"

"What?" Becky tried to keep the shock out of her voice.

"When I wanted to fly down, I called him and he told me he was taking good care of you and not to worry. He said all of you might be coming down this week for vacation. I was so excited to hear that. Your father misses you... I miss you terribly. I thought... well... I..." Her mother broke off in sobs.

It hurt to hear her mother cry. She didn't know what else to say but, "I'm pretty sure the vacation's still on. I'm trying to find someone to fill in for me at work and I can't disappoint the boys. They're looking forward to playing on the beach. So, I guess I'll be there ...maybe."

"That's great!" her mother exclaimed excitedly.

"I said maybe," Becky corrected. Her mother reminded her of the boys. Whenever she said 'maybe' it meant 'yes' in their world.

"I'll tell Dad you'll be here next week. That'll cheer him up. Our good old sunshine could be just what you need. Is it all right with your doctor that you come?"

"I probably should ask first. We might drive versus flying because of all the germs when you're in out in public with other people. I know he mentioned to be careful for a while about exposing myself because the chemo weakened my immune system. Obviously, he forgot what it was like to have children. They're just big germs running around with feet," Becky laughed.

"Driving would be better anyway, dear. No use risking more exposure than necessary. We'll take it easy once you get here." To Becky, her mother sounded like a kid waiting for a Christmas present. A part of her wanted to change her mind and say no, but just hearing her mother's excitement, she couldn't. That would break her heart.

"I guess I might see you soon then," Becky said, "I love you, Mom."

"I love you, honey."

Becky hung up the phone and just stared at it. Now what? She wasn't sure after the conversation she and Kenny had that the invitation was still open for her to accompany him or that he even wanted her to come along. And the work thing was still a huge issue.

❀ ❀ ❀

She met Kenny at a park to exchange the boys. Justin and Adam enjoyed playing while she and Kenny sat on a bench looking like any other married couple to everyone around.

"I talked to Mom…" Becky started the conversation.

"Is your father worse?" Kenny asked with worry. He and her parents had always gotten along great. They loved him as a son and were crushed when she told them about the divorce.

"He's fine."

"It's not your mother's back again, is it?"

"Nope. Her back still hurts, but nothing worse."

"Then why do you sound like something's wrong? I can tell by your voice that things aren't good."

"I… well… I… I kind of promised Mom that I'd tag along with you and the boys on your vacation to Watercolor when you visit them. She wanted to come down during the whole ordeal with the chemo, and I hated to see her fly so I told her no... Now since you're heading there anyway..." She was nervous and couldn't pin down why. What if he said no? She wouldn't blame him because of the way she'd been treating him lately.

"You want to come along with us? I assumed after our last conversation the last thing you wanted to do was spend more time near me."

She supposed she deserved that comment. She swallowed hard. Her pride and fear went down her throat like a clog went down a drain after using Drano.

"I'm sorry. I know you're probably confused. Truth be known, I am too. If it's not too much to ask, I would very much like to go with you and the boys. It would mean a lot to my parents." Becky kicked at the dirt by the bench with her foot.

"What about you? Would it mean a lot to you?" Kenny asked, not quite able to hide the hope springing into his eyes.

"I'm not sure what answer you're looking for, what you want me to say. It would mean a lot to me because I know Mom and Dad would like to see me and the boys... and, of course, you. They're not getting any younger and their health is always a concern. Mom was in her early forties when I was born. I just worry about them, that's all."

He sighed. "Bec, I would love for you to come. Have you checked with your doctor? Can you travel?" Kenny took a deep breath and forced himself to stop questioning her.

"I'm sure it's fine as long as we drive. I know you were planning on flying, but it would be better for me if we didn't. We can drive by the biggest statue of Elvis on our way and show it to the boys."

"I don't mind driving. But are you all right with being in a vehicle that long with me?" Kenny asked with his eyebrows raised.

She smiled and tried to put on a brave face. "I guess I'm going to have to be, aren't I?"

"I guess it shouldn't be a problem if you truly don't have feelings for me anymore." She couldn't tell if he was being serious or teasing her. His tone was flat.

Becky was running out of time for finding someone to fill-in for her while she was gone. She hadn't had a vacation since she started her businesses years ago. She supposed she could see Kenny's view. It would appear that the companies ran her, rather than the other way around.

Desperate, she put in a call to Carmen.

"Hi, Bec, how are you feeling?" Becky could hear the clicking of computer keys in the background.

"I'm feeling tired, but I'm better now that my treatments are over."

"So, what's up? Do you need me to pick up the boys or something?" Carmen asked.

"No, it's nothing like that."

"Well, what is it? You never call me in the middle of the work day. Usually you're too busy," Carmen pointed out. Becky smiled. Her friend was right. She was always busy.

"Can you come down to the pharmacy around two or so?"

"Today?" Carmen asked.

Becky heard Carmen stop typing a mile a minute.

"Yes, today. It's important."

"I'll be there on the dot."

Carmen showed up at two o'clock sharp. Not a second late.

She had that about her. She was always on time and reliable.

"What's up, pharmacist?" Carmen teased.

"Don't you mean what's up doc?" Becky laughed.

"I suppose. I keep forgetting you went back to get your Doctorate in Pharmacy after you were married. I'm always amazed how you raised twins, built your companies and went back to school without anything or anyone suffering," her friend said with pride in her voice.

Becky looked down at her expensive black heels and smoothed her suit. "Sadly, something did suffer—my relationship with my husband."

"I'm sorry. I didn't mean to dredge up old wounds." Carmen put a hand on Becky's shoulder and said in a serious tone, "Why am I here?"

Becky looked at her friend, struggling to find the right words. "You know you're my best friend..."

"I do. We've been friends since before we had bras."

"Well, I had this crazy idea... actually my son had this crazy idea," Becky began.

Carmen nodded for her to continue.

"The idea was that I should hire you to fill in for me and run the business while I'm gone on vacation with them to visit my parents in Florida."

"What?"

"To hire you to run my companies for me," she repeated.

"I heard you. I'm just shocked. Should I be offended that you thought it was a crazy idea?"

"No, it's not like that. I just meant the reason it was crazy was because I didn't think you'd take it. You have a great job now and all," Becky clarified.

"I do have a great job. I make eighty thousand with great benefits," Carmen confirmed. Becky knew she wasn't bragging, just telling it like it was... like she always did. It was a trait that would come in handy training her to run the business.

"Would you consider quitting and coming to work for me? I'd pay you six figures and you'd get three weeks vacation plus bonuses if the business did well under your guidance."

"Bec, I'd work for you for free if you need me to so you can fully recover and take a well-needed rest and relaxation," Carmen said with sincerity in her eyes.

"I would never ask that of you."

"Of course you wouldn't but you're like my sister. Is that what you want? For me to quit my job and run the businesses for you? All you have to do is ask. I'll do it for as long as you need a break and I won't take a dime," her friend told her firmly, planting her hands on her hips.

"Carmen, I admit I do need a break, but not for just a couple of weeks. I need a break completely. I want to hire you to take my place for here on out with good pay... if you want to. Go home and think about it. Talk it over with that sweet husband of yours and tell me when you're ready."

"I'm ready now."

"What?" Becky swallowed the tingle of relief that rose up in her throat. She was sure her friend would say no. It was a silly thought to think she'd want to work for her.

"I say you better start my training, because I'm yours, you silly woman." Carmen smiled.

"Really?"

"Really. I couldn't think of a more honest and sweet boss to work for than you. And don't worry, I'll take good care of the empire you built. I'm excellent at marketing, you know."

"I know. That's what I'm counting on." Becky grinned. Things were coming together just fine. "I have pharmacists working for me who are very skilled, I just need someone to manage the business and marketing aspects like I did."

"Are you sure?" Carmen questioned.

"I'm positive. It's time I stopped to smell the roses... the ones that look like sunsets are my favorite."

"Well, boss. Lead the way."

"I've got a line of customers waiting for me. I don't have time now to train you. When can you start? Next week?" Becky asked as she glanced at the people in line.

"Give me two weeks. I need to give my present job a little notice so I'll be back in two weeks with bells on." Carmen joked and saluted. She gave Becky a quick hug and then hurried away.

Becky let out a sigh. She turned to a customer and was about to ask if she could help when the phone rang. She picked it up on the third ring. She had three customers waiting for prescriptions and one irate customer demanding in a loud voice that she renew his pain medicine two weeks before the insurance company would allow.

"Yes?" she said briskly into the phone.

"Mrs. Winroy?"

"Yes?" Becky grabbed a prescription off the shelf for the next person in line as she waited for a reply.

"Your husband was brought in by ambulance a short time ago. He's in critical condition. He's sustained a head injury and some broken ribs…"

"What?" she asked weakly, her heart in her throat. Her hands were shaking so badly she nearly dropped the phone. She felt like someone just punched her in the stomach and knocked the wind right out of her.

"Your husband, Kenny Winroy. We're not sure he's going to make it so you might want to get to the hospital…"

"My boys?" Becky asked in a panic, looking up at the clock. It was time for Kenny to take them to practice. They had to be in the car as well.

"Your boys were in the car."

"Oh, dear God. Are they…?" Becky felt herself sway and grabbed the edge of the counter to keep herself upright.

"No, your husband swerved to miss a truck that ran a stop sign and he turned the vehicle so that he took the worst of the impact," the man told her. "Your kids have a few bumps and bruises, nothing more."

"I'll be right there," Becky promised as the prescription fell from her hands and landed on the floor with a clink.

She looked at all the people waiting, hung up the phone and quickly informed them, "I'm sorry the store is closing early due to a family emergency."

She heard the disgruntled man wanting his pain medicine early curse loudly as the rest of the crowd murmured in understanding. She grabbed her keys and gave orders to the technician. "Close up for me. I'm going to the hospital to see my husband."

"I thought you were divorced?" the technician asked in confusion as Becky walked out the door.

She called out over her shoulder, "Technically, I am."

Becky arrived at the hospital in record time, the urgency to reach her family, overwhelming. The fear building in her chest that Kenny would be gone by the time she reached him was a terror she never thought she'd feel. The voice on the phone had sounded like she didn't have time to waste. Time seemed to be the underlined theme lately.

Time. She needed more of it.

Becky had called Carmen and Andrea as she drove, informing them of the accident. She needed her friends yet again to watch the boys.

The boys. Thank God, they weren't hurt. She didn't know what she would do if anything happened to them.

She whipped her vehicle into a hospital parking space. Becky's heart pumped rapidly as she ran across the asphalt to reach the emergency room doors. This was the most exercise she had, well… since before she was diagnosed with cancer. Thankfully, her body didn't fail her like before.

Carmen was waiting for her at the entrance. Becky asked out of breath, "How did you get here so fast?"

"I had a few minutes head start than you."

"Have you seen Adam or Justin yet?" Becky looked around frantically as if expecting to see them sitting on a chair in the lobby.

"No, I was waiting for you."

Becky rushed toward the information desk, unsure

where Kenny was and needed to ask. The volunteer checked her computer then explained Kenny was in ICU, informing Becky she could see him for just a second, letting her know he was in a coma and hadn't wakened since the accident.

Becky nodded and turned toward Carmen. "I'll be right back. Can you find the boys?"

"Sure. No problem."

She hurried toward the elevator and punched the button to take her up to the fourth floor where the intensive care units were. When she walked into ICU where Kenny was, she shattered. Bits and pieces of her own stay started to flash through her mind. The smell. The machines. The constant beeps. She eyed the empty chair next to the bed and an image of Kenny sitting there while she'd been sick vividly appeared. She couldn't get his unshaven reddish beard, tousled hair and worried face out of her mind.

Her gaze finally found its way to where Kenny lay in the bed. She didn't want to see him like this and had been glancing everywhere but at him. She swallowed back the hard knots lining up like soldiers in her throat.

Kenny's head was bandaged and she could tell from the sheets that had slipped down his body that his ribs were also wrapped. Black and blue discolorations marred his handsome face and scratches were embedded into his skin.

Becky had to force her feet to move to the bed. Glancing down at Kenny, she immediately became dizzy and light-headed, bile filling her throat. She wanted to run. She wanted to stay. Crazy mixed-up emotions tumbled through her head. She sat down on the side of the bed and took Kenny's hand in her own, her heart aching with the need to say the things she knew she shouldn't say.

She whispered, "So, this is what it feels like to love someone and not know if they'll be coming back to you. This is the pain and agony of love."

Becky stroked the roughness of his beard a moment, then leaned in and kissed where her fingers had touched.

She felt her throat swell with panic and swallowed it down.

She picked up his left hand and ran a fingertip across the wedding band he still wore and whispered through the tears flowing down her face, "I love you, Kenny."

She thought she felt his fingers move, but when she examined his features and the monitors, nothing had changed.

The nurse entered. "Time to go, Mrs. Winroy. You can sit in the waiting room with your boys and friends, if you like."

"My boys?" Becky smiled in relief.

"Yes," the nurse answered as she checked a few buttons and then walked out.

Becky found herself nearly running to the waiting area. She saw Carmen, Adam, Justin and Andrea all sitting there waiting.

"Justin! Adam!" Becky ran with her arms wide open.

The boys rushed to her and she wrapped them in her embrace. They all sobbed out their relief.

"Lady ran stop sign…" Justin got out between hiccups.

"Is Daddy going to die?" Adam managed between tears.

Becky touched both of their cheeks. Each appeared to be uninjured, which was a miracle. "Daddy will be just fine. He's strong and will be just fine."

Her own words sounded weak to her ears. She only hoped the boys didn't notice.

"Why don't I take you to get a snack out of the vending machine?" Andrea asked holding out her hands.

The boys moved to her and for a moment looked like kids again. "I want chocolate," Adam said.

"I want chips," Justin answered.

After they walked away, Carmen stood up and took Becky in her arms. "Are you all right?"

"I'm… I don't know. Seeing him lying there… it was so hard."

"Would you be any other place than here with him?" Carmen asked as she wiped a tear away from her friend's cheek.

"No."

"Would you trade loving him to take away this moment of pain?" Carmen pressed.

"No."

"Then I think you have the answer you've been searching for since you were diagnosed with cancer. There are no guarantees for any of us and the joy of loving someone far outweighs the pain of losing them," her friend said as she adjusted Becky's scarf around her head. She still wore it because there wasn't much hair yet and it was coming in curly and funny-looking.

Becky slipped to her knees and sobbed. "I've wasted so much time. If only I would've told him how I felt about him before... before..."

"He knows how you feel and he's not going to die," she insisted. "You told the boys that he's strong. Was that a lie?"

Was it? She had to tell the boys something so they wouldn't worry and from the looks of sympathy on the nurses' faces, Becky wasn't sure he was going to make it. The certainty that she may lose him caused her to sob that much harder. Carmen sat next to her on the cold hospital floor for what seemed like hours, but in reality were only minutes.

Finally after all her tears were spent, Becky looked up and wiped a hand across her nose, giving an unlady-like sniff. "He made me a mix of songs to listen to during the MRI test to help me with my claustrophobia."

Carmen didn't say anything, just sat and listened as Becky continued, "If it wasn't for those songs... I would've clawed my way out of that machine." She sighed and hiccupped. "You know what the strangest part about the tape was?"

"What?" Carmen asked softly, rubbing a hand in circles over her best friend's back.

"Those songs brought back all of those memories of us

together... from the song I played to him on a dare to the song from our wedding. All those sweet tortuous memories. It was that tape that made those buried feelings start to stir."

"You were never out of love with him, you know that. I'm guessing those songs just reminded you of the reasons you loved him in the first place. I have to hand it to Kenny for being supportive, determined to get you back and being romantic all at once," Carmen said wisely.

"What have I done, Carmen? What have I done? I've wasted so much time. Time that I might not get a chance to make up. What if he..." Becky started to cry again.

"He'll wake up. You woke up. Miracles do happen, you know. You're proof of that. God has plenty of miracles up his sleeves yet. Just have faith and hope and believe in your love."

"What about our divorce? What about all the reasons we got divorced?" Becky tried to hang on to reasoning.

"Those irreconcilable differences are now reconciled. End of argument. Just let it all go and start from this moment on... for your family's sake. They need you."

The nurse hurried over to where they sat on the floor. "Your husband is asking for you."

"What?" Becky exclaimed in shock, not knowing what to do or say since Kenny wasn't her husband. Should she tell the nurse that fact?

"Go see your husband," Carmen urged, waving her on, "he needs you."

Becky sprang to her feet and followed the nurse.

"Make sure you don't excite him or upset him in any way," the nurse advised. "He still has a long road to recovery."

Fourteen

Becky had her hand on the handle of the truck. It seemed lately she'd been spending a lot of time in this truck of her ex-husband's. It reminded her of the time she was standing on the high dive trying to decide to jump or not to jump while all the kids were watching, waiting for her to be brave or chicken. Becky opened the door to the truck—she was no chicken.

"Ready?" Kenny asked as if knowing exactly what she was struggling with.

"Sure." Becky acted confident, playing the part, telling herself she should've been an actress. "Are you sure you don't want me to drive? It's only been a few weeks since you've been out of the hospital," Becky pointed out.

"The doctor cleared me to drive to Florida. I'm completely better... minus a little tenderness in my ribs yet," Kenny said touching his side.

"It's hard to believe we've been in the hospital and both had something wrong with our heads," Becky commented.

"Yes, I guess God was trying to knock some sense into both of us the hard way," Kenny laughed.

"Hey, Mom, can we stop to eat?" Adam asked.

"Your grandparents are eagerly waiting for us to get

there. We are a few weeks behind our visit because of your father's recovery. How about one of the snacks I packed instead?" Becky smiled and threw him a pack of crackers.

"Thanks, Mom."

They played all kinds of car games—spot the alphabet on signs and license plates, find every state on the license plate, and, of course, the fun car bingo game she'd bought. Kenny had been driving for three hours and she felt fatigue washing over her. Her stamina wasn't quite what it was before her bout with cancer. She slid a movie into the DVD player for the boys—you had to love portable DVD players, she mused silently and then rested her head against the seat. This wasn't as bad as she thought it would be. To be honest, it actually was fun. She found herself enjoying the time she'd been spending with Kenny lately and as a family. It felt good.

"Sleepy?" Kenny asked as he placed a hand on her thigh.

She wanted to pull away, but didn't want to draw attention with the boys in the backseat.

"A little," she admitted.

"Go to sleep. The boys are happy and I'm fine to drive."

She nodded her thanks and tilted her head to lean against the cold hard window. She should've remembered to bring a pillow along, she told herself as she took a deep breath. She was so tired it really didn't seem to matter how hard the object was her head rested against. Becky found herself drifting off to a place of peaceful darkness.

When she woke, she felt softness beneath her head. She frowned, trying to determine what it was. It sure didn't feel like the hard surface of a window. Becky raised her eyes slowly and found herself staring at Kenny's strong jaw.

"Umm…" Becky muttered as she pushed herself into a sitting position. What should she say?

"Have a good nap?" Kenny asked casually.

"Yes… I… somehow drifted over to your side. I'm sorry."

"Don't be sorry. The window didn't look too comfortable anyway. I'm glad you did. It was nice having your head on my shoulder again. It's been a long time"

Kenny gave her a quick look and then forced his attention back to the road. She couldn't tell from that split-second glance what he was thinking.

"Are we almost there?" Becky asked.

"Yep. We just entered Watercolor. If I remember correctly your parent's house is just a few blocks from the resort area."

Sadly, she hadn't visited but one time since their move to Florida. She came when her dad had surgery just for two days. It had been Kenny's turn with the kids and she'd flown down on a Friday night and flew back on a Sunday night. She couldn't miss work. It's strange now how quickly that loyalty faded. She'd missed out on so much with that kind of thinking. Some might say she had the luxury of thinking of working less and playing more because her businesses were very lucrative. However, even when she and Kenny were just starting off and could barely put food on the table and pay the rent, she still worked long hours. She worked long hours when they were poor so she could stop working long hours and enjoy life later on, but when she finally got to that point where she could've worked less, she didn't. It was a different excuse then to work. Instead of the reason of being hungry, it became the reason of wanting to have money in savings 'just in case.' Then when she had money in savings for 'just in case,' it became she wanted to start saving for family vacations—not that she would've taken off work for them. There always seemed to be one reason or another to work. Now she had a reason not to, she knew how precious life was.

"What are you thinking about?" Kenny asked. "You seem so deep in thought and you have a frown on your face. Aren't you having a good time with me?"

"It's not that. I'm having a great time with you. I just wish that I would've known years ago what I finally figured out now. Not to take life for granted, how very precious it is."

"That it is. That it is," Kenny agreed with a nod.

"Don't you wish we could've done more with the boys when they were young? Perhaps, did certain things differently?"

"They're still young. Goodness, they're only seven." Kenny laughed in amusement. "But I know what you mean. I guess every parent thinks that way—that they wish they would've savored more of their kid's lives."

"You think so?" Becky asked, uncertain if what he said was true.

"I think so. Everyone is running the race together in this fast-paced world. You can't completely quit the race even if you want to. Things cost money and you get money from working. I guess there just has to be a happy medium of working and playing." He reached over and touched the hand lying in her lap. "What do you wish you would've done differently?"

"I regret not showing you more how much I loved you. People told me the relationship between husband and wife is more important than the relationship with your kids. I just didn't believe them. Now I understand. If you let that deteriorate, the stability and family unit is at risk of falling apart. I think we're proof of that. I thought if I put all of my energy into the kids then everything would be fine, and I was wrong. Everything wasn't fine."

"It's not too late to make things right," Kenny said softly.

"I guess not. But we've changed. I'm not the same Becky that you used to know and you're not the same Kenny I used to know."

"I'm sure that's true," Kenny agreed quietly. "But beneath all those changes is still the girl I fell in love with and who's still the mother of my children. I think that gives us a pretty good foundation already for making this thing work.

How about you just open up your heart and mind on this vacation and give me a chance to know you again, changes and all, and we'll see where that takes us. No pressures. Just dating."

"Just dating? Isn't that odd considering we were once married?" Becky asked doubtfully.

"Does it matter how odd it is? Who cares how odd or unusual it is. Your parents will be wanting to spend time with their beloved grandchildren. It'll be the perfect opportunity to use them to baby-sit while we go on a few dates. What do you say? Will you go on a date with me?" Kenny asked, swinging his sweet puppy gaze her way.

"You remind me of a dog looking out through the bars at a pound begging for someone to take him home."

"Should I be offended you just compared me to a dog?" Kenny chuckled.

"No," she smiled and found herself giving in, "I guess a few dates won't hurt anything. Only if we keep it under wraps from the kids. I don't want to give them false hope that their parents might get back together only to have their hearts crushed again."

"Deal," Kenny grinned, "No false hope."

Becky adjusted her red slip dress. It was the same one she'd worn over her swimsuit at the birthday party. She'd noticed then Kenny had seemed to like it, and for some reason she couldn't help herself from wearing it again. It was a purchase she'd made a year ago. A pharmacy sales representative came in and after a long discussion, he'd asked her out. She'd had a moment of vulnerability and said yes. She rushed out shopping after work and chose this dress. However, when she put it on that night and looked in the mirror, it hadn't felt right, so she yanked off the dress and called her prospective date, telling him she'd made a mistake and she was sorry. He was very understanding. The little red dress had been sitting in her closet ever since—until Blake's birthday party. It had sent out a beacon to her that night, just like it was doing this night.

When she walked out onto her parent's huge porch, Kenny and her dad were sitting in chairs talking. She had to admit her parents always loved him. She overheard something about fishing and had to smile. Her dad was going on about fishing in the lake down the street. They looked up and ceased their conversation when she walked over. Kenny immediately stood up and she could hear the intake of his breath.

She found herself smiling. "I hope this is appropriate for where we're going tonight."

"It's perfect," Kenny stated in a husky tone.

Her father cleared his throat and Becky blushed in embarrassment. "Sorry, Dad. I guess we should get going. Thanks for watching the boys."

"No problem. We miss them now that we live so far away. You two go off and have a good time." Her dad eyed Kenny with a serious face. "Have my daughter back by eleven."

Kenny's eyes grew large at his statement and smiled. "Good one, Dad. You sounded for a moment like you did when Bec and I first dated decades ago."

He ignored Kenny's remark, not budging on his seriousness. "Eleven. Not a minute later."

At first, Becky thought he was joking too, but there wasn't even a hint of a smile on his face. "Oh, Dad."

"Don't 'oh Dad' me. You just got through with intensive chemotherapy treatments and need your rest. Eleven o'clock or I'll sic your mother on you. Besides, Kenny just got out of the hospital as well for a serious car accident. Something about a coma ring a bell?"

Becky glanced at Kenny and he nodded. "Yes, Dad. I'll have her back not a minute past eleven. You have my word."

"Good, son. I know I can count on your word and that we both care about Becky's health and love her."

"Dad, I'm standing right here in front of you. You're talking like I'm not even here," Becky scolded.

"Sorry, dear." Her dad's face softened as he looked at her. "Enjoy the evening."

Kenny offered his arm and she linked hers through his. He assisted her down the steps to his truck. That truck again, she mused.

Their date turned out to be a fabulous occasion. They ate at a restaurant overlooking the ocean. It was beautiful. The sunset framed them as they sipped their coffee and ate cheesecake.

"I don't think my doctor would approve of me eating cheesecake. He was pretty strict about nutrition and how it went hand-in-hand with this whole process," Becky said with a sigh as she put the last delicious lemon-flavored morsel into her mouth. It melted on her tongue like a snowflake and she moaned in pleasure.

Kenny grinned. "I just decided what I want to come back as if we're able to be recycled."

She laughed at his reference to reincarnation. "And what is that?"

"A piece of lemon cheesecake on your plate." Kenny couldn't help but laugh after the words were out of his mouth.

"I think it would fit since right now you sound cheesy." Becky shook her head, unable to believe such a line.

"Okay. Okay. I apologize, but it came from the heart."

"Uh, huh. I'm sure it did." Becky laughed in amusement, knowing full well where that comment came from.

"Are you up to the next stage of our date?" Kenny asked, smoothing into the next subject.

"You know you have to have me home by eleven or meet the wrath of my father, remember?"

"I do. I'll have you home in plenty of time," Kenny assured her.

"Okay, then, where are we going?"

Kenny paid the bill and pushed to his feet, walking around to pull out her chair. He'd become so much more thoughtful over these past couple of years, she found herself thinking, pleased that he was doing so.

"We're going to a café two blocks down to sit outside under the stars and sip our coffee then listen to a local band," Kenny explained as he led her out of the restaurant.

Becky glanced back over her shoulder. "You know, I think this was one of the best places I've ever eaten."

"*Fish Out of Water* is known for its good food, but I love to hear the waves wash over the sand. To me that's priceless," Kenny said as they made their way over the boardwalk and onto the street.

"I didn't know you were this romantic."

"I guess you can teach an old dog a new trick," Kenny chuckled and added, "But this dog has his tail tucked for not knowing better all along and learning the tricks on his own. I should've done research on how to be a better husband. There are tons of books out there on that topic. I should've just swallowed my pride and bought a few—like that book *Men are from Mars and Women are from Venus.*"

"I heard the *Multi Orgasmic Woman* is a great read as well," Becky teased.

Kenny's head turned so fast she thought he looked like the girl in the *Exorcist*. She laughed, "Sorry, I forgot this was our first date."

"Don't be sorry. I think I know what to buy the next time I'm at the book store." Kenny smiled and took her hand in his as they walked. Somehow it no longer felt awkward, it just felt right. They'd crossed back over that line and it was nicer on this side.

"I'm sorry for pushing you away. I thought you deserved more than to be involved with a woman who might die at any point in the future." Becky couldn't meet his eyes, instead stared down at her sandals.

"Becky, any one of us can die at any time, I'm proof of that. I almost died in that car accident and I wasn't the one who had cancer. We're all here for a limited amount of time. It can be one day or a hundred days or one hundred years. The important thing is to make the best of it and love freely and passionately."

"I want to love freely and passionately just as much as you do," Becky said, moisture swimming in her eyes.

"I love you, Becky. I always have and always will," Kenny said as he cupped her chin in his hand and brushed her lips with his own. She grew warm, felt passion stir and tingled from the sensation. His lips were so soft.

"Let's get you to that outdoor concert, otherwise I don't foresee having you home by eleven. I'll instead have you on the beach somewhere…"

Becky blushed at his meaning.

Somehow the next several days were just a whirlwind. Kenny was always by her side or with her and the boys. It was so much better than before the divorce. She laughed at his dry sense of humor and he laughed at her silly antics. Each time she paused for a second and observed the boys, she found them beaming with happiness. She and Kenny were trying to keep their dates a secret, but whatever was growing between them was happening so fast she was sure they picked up on it.

As Kenny picked her up in his arms and spun her around in circles on the beach, Justin watched with interest. "Mom, are you in love with Dad again?"

Kenny stopped what he was doing and slowly set her back on her feet. Becky knew her mouth must be open wide in shock. She wasn't sure what to say. Should she confirm she was or deny it?

Thankfully, Kenny saved her. "Why don't you boys

grab the Frisbee out of the beach bag and we'll all toss it around. Your mother has quite an arm and a great catch."

Fortunately, Justin fell for the distraction. "Yeah, Dad, I think she's better at sports than you."

"I'm crushed." Kenny placed a hand over his chest, acting as if he'd been shot and fell to the sand in a mock death.

Adam agreed with Justin. "I think you'll be the first one to drop the Frisbee, Dad. I'm betting on Mom."

"I'll take that bet." Kenny jumped to his feet, saluting like a soldier as Justin ran to get the plastic disk.

Becky leaned over and whispered in Kenny's ear, "Should I drop it so you can win the bet and save face in front of your boys?"

"Why I ought to…" Kenny started to chase her in mock anger. Becky zigzagged out of the way like she was dribbling down a basketball court.

"You ought to what?" Becky challenged, executing a spin move, faking left then right. "Lose?"

Kenny managed to catch up with her because exhaustion was claiming her after just a few minutes. "No fair, I haven't gotten my stamina back yet." She was huffing and puffing for air.

She could tell Kenny was about to say something serious. A worried look appeared on his features, but Adam prevented him from doing so when he ran up with the glow-in-the-dark Frisbee. "Game on!"

As she walked by Kenny to her spot for the game, she whispered in a soft tone, "I'm fine, so stop with the worrying if you want to make this work. You've got to just live one day at a time with me. Besides, you shouldn't overdo it as well, Mr. Coma."

Adam threw the Frisbee at his father and just as Kenny was about to grab it, a gust of wind kicked up and the disk went right past his fingers and hit the sand.

"I think Dad lost the bet!" Adam yelled as he fell into

the sand. "On the first throw."

Kenny waited for her down the beach, Becky smiling as she walked toward him. Somehow, she'd found her way back to where she belonged. She realized that cancer hadn't been her enemy after all, but a gift... a gift from God. Through her sickness she'd found what was most important. Her family.

The soft strains of Mozart drifted over the sounds of the waves. The ocean seemed to be in harmony to the already perfect music. Her dress blew around her in the warm breeze as she moved down the beach to where Kenny was waiting. Seashells crunched under her sandals and the smell of roses mated with the salted air. When Becky stood next to Kenny, she smoothed the rainbow scarf tied around her head, trying to keep it in place despite the wind. She no longer needed it, she knew, but it had become symbolic of where she came from and of Kenny.

Father Joe smiled at the couple. "We come here today for the marriage of these two people..."

Tears formed in her eyes when Father said the words 'in sickness and in health, 'till death do us part.' The words had a whole new meaning this time around. She looked on as Kenny took her hand in his and answered with tears filling his own eyes, "I do."

She realized then how lucky she was to find true love twice in a lifetime, for she loved Kenny the first time as a woman-child loves and she loved Kenny this time as a woman loves. Becky couldn't help but give the biggest smile when Father Joe pronounced them man and wife for a second time. Kenny swept her up in his arms and gave her the biggest, most passionate kiss.

"I'm never letting you go again, Mrs. Winroy."

"I'm never letting you go again, Mr. Winroy."

Alone in their room, Becky smiled at her husband. She could feel the pent up emotions and sexual energy between them. Energy that had been denied for much too long. This time when he approached her, she didn't protest. This time he wasn't unsure. Kenny swept her up in his arms and carried her toward the bed. She looked over her shoulder.

He read her mind, knew what she was thinking. "The boys went over to your parent's house. They won't be back until dinnertime."

Her thoughts ran to whether or not she had the energy to do what he was asking. Taking those few running steps on the beach and playing Frisbee felt like she'd played full court basketball for an hour.

"I'll be gentle and slow," Kenny murmured in a husky whisper. They'd never been this in-tuned before. In the past, he'd never seemed to know what she needed or wanted, yet lately he appeared to know exactly what it was that she craved. That realization frightened her.

"Kenny, I don't know if getting married again was such a good idea. What if I'm not in remission after all and my cancer isn't gone? What if the chemo didn't take care of it? This is too much of a risk to take. We shouldn't be doing this. You shouldn't be doing this. It's like gambling on a horse that might not make it to the finish line."

He stopped walking and looked down into her eyes. He tipped her chin up with his forefinger. "I'm a gambling man and my heart is on you. I know you'll make it. How can you not? You're strong and spunky and damn stubborn to boot. I love you and regardless of the outcome, I want to experience the ride."

"Ken?" She reverted back to what she called him in the past.

"No, stop thinking and just let me love you. Let me rediscover every inch of your body again and this time, the way it should've always been loved and cherished. I've changed, let me show you how much."

His lips didn't allow her to answer. She felt his warm mouth caressing hers and forgot about all the other excuses she had for not doing what both of them wanted to do. She forgot about being sick. She forgot about his near death experience. She forgot about everything. For the first time in her entire life she just lived in the moment and didn't analyze and didn't question or worry. She just lived.

True to his word, he discovered places he'd never uncovered before. There wasn't a place on her body that wasn't kissed and caressed. By the time his lips came back to meet hers she was floating into another dimension, trembling with the fulfillment that only came from unselfish loving and giving.

As he pulled himself slightly above her, she vaguely wondered what he was going to do next, her mind still full of the way he'd just loved her. Kenny removed the only clothing she had left on her body—her scarf. Reality came back and she cried out in horror, "No!"

"Let me love all of you."

"No..." Becky protested, now feeling vulnerable and uncertain. "It's not the same anymore."

"Let me, Bec, let me," Kenny begged with love in his eyes.

She stared up into his cyan-colored eyes and for a moment was afraid she'd drown if she took a step forward into the unknown, but then she dove in, just wanting to go back to that feeling of tranquility and peace washing over her again. Kenny dropped her scarf and started to slowly kiss her head. Hair was growing back in, but the lush curvy hair he was used to was not there.

"I don't have beautiful hair anymore. What I do have is coarse and not as soft," Becky stated, her voice cracking with sadness.

"When I look at you, I've never seen you look so stunning. You don't need a certain type of hair to make yourself beautiful. The beauty I see in you, that I've always seen in you, comes from your heart and your soul. It's the way you laugh when you're playing tag with the boys. It's the giggle you have when playing hide and seek and can't quite keep silent in your awesome hiding spot. The radiance you emit when you talk about the boys and your work. The passion with which you tackled basketball, with not wanting to accept defeat. All of those things are what makes you stunning."

Tears streamed down her face and dripped off her chin. Kenny lowered his head to kiss away her tears. Involuntarily, her eyes drifted over the length his body as he drew back. He had the most toned and muscular body of any model or athlete, but for the first time ever she didn't look at the muscles that defined him, she looked at the character and essence that made him who he was. What she saw took her breath away. He was truly beautiful.

"Ken..." She reached up to lay a hand over his heart.

"I feel what you're feeling. I've always heard about people connecting on a spiritual plane, but I never knew it existed. It's like I'm seeing you in a light that just warms and fills every empty space in my body and heart."

"I know. Now I know what people who are in love feel when they're ninety. It's a love that sees past all the physical and instead sees directly into the heart, mind and soul," Becky whispered as she looked at Kenny poised above her.

"Becky?"

She welcomed him back into her body and her heart.

Epilogue

Twenty years later

"Where's Justin?" Becky asked as she glanced around the church.

"I don't know. How should I know?" Adam said, shrugging his broad shoulders and running a hand through his red hair.

"Because you're the best man that's why," Becky pointed out to her son.

"Yeah, but I was busy feeding Amanda and lost track of him," Adam defended himself.

"I guess that's a good enough excuse." Becky smiled at the mention of her first grandchild.

"Why don't you give me that delicious little baby and go find your brother and make sure he's fine." Becky held out her arms and Adam placed the sleeping infant gently into his grandmother's embrace.

"All right, but if you see my wife, tell her where I went."

"How's my wonderful daughter-in-law doing?" Becky smiled at the mention of Pamela.

"She's worn out. She had a long week performing surgeries. It always amazes me how she can keep going with a family and work."

"That's because Pamela has such a great husband helping her," Becky beamed with pride. "Staying at home with your children is hard but a blessing. It probably can be even harder than doing a surgery. I'm so proud that you're a stay-at-home dad."

"Thanks. Sometimes I'm afraid I'll get teased for it or people will think that I'm no-good, letting my wife support me," Adam admitted as she took a blanket out of the diaper bag he was holding and placed it over his sleeping little girl.

"You're the most masculine man I know, next to your father, of course." Becky leaned down and kissed the pudgy little cheek of her granddaughter.

"Somehow I went from making six figures as an investment broker to changing dozens of diapers overnight." Adam's laugh was amused. "But I don't miss my old life at all."

Becky nodded, understanding perfectly well what he meant. She didn't regret for one minute choosing to have Carmen run her companies. The pharmacies had expanded and grown under her leadership and guidance. Five more stores had been opened over the past two decades and when that happened, Becky had made Carmen an equal partner.

Andrea walked up and made silly happy faces at the baby. "I miss that stage."

Becky laughed in agreement. "Me, too. I guess we have to live vicariously through our children now."

Her friend nodded. "All the flowers are ready. I think I'm starting to feel like I'm in a rose parade."

"I know, but you know Chloe. She loves roses. She wanted every color available at her wedding."

"Every rose but the rose that's yours and Kenny's," Andrea teased and pulled out a corsage. "I've got explicit instructions to give the mother of the groom this before the ceremony."

"It's beautiful." Becky lifted the flower up to her nose

and breathed in.

"Kenny said the Tahitian Sunset Rose is the rose that should be given to the mother of the groom." Andrea glanced around and then whispered, "He's so romantic."

"I have to agree. These twenty years have been the best years of my life, not only am I still cancer-free but I'm living a life that is very blessed."

"Well, you better put that corsage on, because the wedding is going to start soon. Where is Justin anyway?" Andrea looked around worriedly.

"I don't know. That's just where I was heading," Becky said and then added, "You did a great job with the flowers, Andrea."

"Thanks. It started out as a hobby while the kids were little and ended up being my passion and my job."

"You've made a very awesome cosmetic and perfume line using the flowers as well. Who would've thought a floral and cosmetic store together in one?" Becky commented.

"It's all thanks to clients like you and now I'm thinking of expanding."

"Don't tell Kenny that. He'll think we went overboard on the flowers." Becky glanced around hoping Kenny didn't overhear.

"You get the best friend and mother of the bride discount so I think the total is free."

"I've already told you I'd split the cost with you," Becky admonished.

"No, this is my gift to my baby girl. Besides, I'm just so happy she's marrying Justin. They've been dating since they were young, they remind me of you and Kenny."

"Then they're very blessed to have the love that we have. Very blessed indeed," Becky said touching her wedding ring. Kenny had it resized for their wedding on the beach. It now fit her finger again and more importantly, her heart.

"We better run Justin down so we can get this wedding

started and before Chloe has a nervous breakdown." Andrea waved Becky on.

Becky searched everywhere. Finally, she checked outside by the benches and found Justin sitting there alone. She sat down next to her son and asked, "Is everything okay, dear?"

Justin didn't answer for a second and then asked in a quiet voice, "Mom, what if Chloe gets sick like you did? What if she even dies? I love her so much. I don't think I could handle losing her. I could barely handle almost losing you. You know her grandmother died of breast cancer and it can run in the family."

Becky sat in shock at her son's words. She didn't know he still had such strong emotions toward her sickness and struggles. She curved an arm around his waist. "Justin, life is filled with uncertainty, but one thing you can be sure of is if you don't take a chance, you'll never get the wonderful rewards it has to offer. The best reward of all was loving your father all these years. We never know how long we have on this earth, but you can't live in fear. It's not healthy and it's lonely. I was so lonely those couple of years I was apart from your father."

"But you had us."

"Yes, I had you, which was wonderful, but a part of me was missing without your father. I'm just blessed that I came to my senses and figured it out. In a strange way, I have my illness to thank for that. It ended up being one of the best things that ever happened to me as scary and hard as it was. I learned to live again in the midst of not knowing if I was going to live or die," Becky said, wiping a tear from her eye.

"I love you, Mom."

"I love you too, Justin. Now go have many years of happiness with the woman of your dreams," Becky told him with misty eyes.

"Thanks, Mom. Thank you for being such a wonderful

mother all these years. You and Dad were great parents."

Becky felt her heart swell with love, her chest fill with pride. She was so very blessed. She was given the gift of watching her children grow and become adults, get married and even see her first grandchild when she wasn't sure she'd even see them through to their fourth grade. Life was filled with glorious gifts and joyous surprises. Becky sniffed the sweet lickerish smell of the Tahitian Sunset Rose corsage decorating her wrist and sighed with contentment.

She looked up to heaven and whispered, "Thank you, God, for the gift of life and the gift of beautiful sunsets."

Stacey Lynn Schlegl has a BS in biology from Maryville University and graduated Magna Cum Laude. She is a mother of two small children and volunteers her time as a librarian, room mother, fundraising activities, and running the re-sale shop PTL committee at her children's school. She has published various series in romance and non-fiction. To learn more about this author, visit her website at www.SLSromance.co

Printed in the United States
136422LV00001B/3/P